A MIRAGE IN THE MEMORY

A PREQUEL TO THE SLIP SAGA

SIMON TULL

ULTRALUMINAL

For Sylvie

… even though it's not the book you wanted.

CHAPTER
ONE

Most immortals didn't believe memories could kill. Thibault Allard knew different.

Memories etched wounds worse than any acid, scarring the mind with the residues of reality. Like medicating with methadone, memories paled in comparison to the real thing, every recollection a potential of further corruption.

Thibault ran a chrome thumb over his hard plastic headgear. The nanofilm on the digit signalled the ridges of the stowed electrodes, each one a promise of another place. In his other hand, he thumbed a chit, a small disc reminiscent of an old poker chip.

Ors wheeled over in his office chair, rollers clacking on the crumbling linoleum. Neon-blue lights cast soft shadows over his ancient burns and melted flesh, the crevices crafting a dark cobalt lattice on his skin.

"What's it going to be?" Ors' ragged vocal cords fought the background hum of fans and computers crowding his place.

Thibault hesitated, squeezing the mesh. His hand trembled. He met Ors' lidless gaze, trying to ignore the pus weeping down the man's cheek, staining the collar of a once-white business shirt. "I don't understand. Why couldn't you track the sender?"

"I figure they exited after they pinged me." Ors sounded irritated. "Either that, or they have skills I've never seen before."

"Not likely."

The scarred vire shrugged. "The night you think you know it all . . ."

The mysterious message glowed in backlit characters on one of the many screens—a paltry few words given the significance they imparted.

[I have information about Marina Allard. Tell the hunter to meet me in Aurora.]

Thibault stared at the glimmering text. Who knew that he was searching for his wife, apart from Ors? Before seeing this message, Thibault would have said no one. How many more knew his secret?

The chit in his hand weighed heavier than a black hole. "What do you think?"

Ors gave him a strange look, bulging eyeballs swivelling in their sockets. "Someone offers you a thread of hope when you'd all but given up? You can't be thinking to ignore it."

Thibault said nothing for a moment, clutching the chit hard, feeling it bite into his palm. "It's my last one."

"Ah."

One last chit. With it, he could ease back into the stiff foam of the pod, settle the mesh onto his scalp, let the electrodes plumb his brain matter, and see Marina again. Enter the neural echo coded by Ors from Thibault's recollections, so he might live a digital lie with her, for as long as his chits lasted.

But every time he meshed, those memories decayed a little more, became a little more fragmented. Too large for Ors to fit in external storage, forcing them to be streamed on each visitation. So each time, the echo morphed again, Thibault's mind striving to fill in the gaps until he couldn't recall the truth anymore.

Ors had warned him. Thibault hadn't listened.

One last venture into the slip, into his memories, and then . . . what? Would the great vire hunter Thibault Allard once again chase bounties for the Trinity, stalk the lost and the damned, no matter the tar it stuck to his soul? He'd started to believe he could be better than that, though perhaps that was simply another lie.

Ors interrupted his thoughts. "It's not the chit holding you back."

"What do you mean?"

"You're afraid."

"Afraid?" Thibault ground out the word.

Ors nodded at the screen. "Afraid to hope. To hope it might be true."

Thibault swallowed, his throat suddenly dry. Ors wasn't wrong. Dangerous, resurrecting a dead hope. Hope could scorch you to dust faster than the sun's vees. But what did the hopeless have to lose?

Thibault opened his hand and stared at the chit. Scratches marred the surface, so numerous that no part of it appeared untouched. For something so worthless to mean so much . . . he could almost see Fate's middle finger inscribed in the plastic.

Thibault had never asked Ors for a free ride, and he wasn't about to start. Ors used his funds to bribe Trinity enforcers to look the other way, and with three Families in play, it amounted to a hefty fee.

Ors cut in again. "That echo will drive you mad, Tibs. I've seen it before. The past should stay in the past. Look to the future instead." He paused. "So what'll it be? Marina, or Aurora?"

Thibault clenched his hands, metal fingers digging into metal palms. It was no choice, not really. A chance to see Marina again? No choice at all.

"Aurora."

Memories flooded in at the word. Old memories of blood and sweat and need. Even the mention of the dawnclub had his Thirst restless in its slumber.

Ors studied him. "Can you handle it?"

"I can handle it, kin." Thibault's voice inflected at the end, betraying his uncertainty. He settled the plastic mesh onto his head, the magnets on the band bonding with the plugs dotting his skull. His crown quivered with trace vibrations, embedded ports sliding open, exposing the brain tissue within.

Marina's face flashed by, longing and lonely. How could he be sure that face was even hers anymore?

Ors swivelled to the backlit panel by Thibault's pod and tapped the screen with printless fingers. "I'll drop you out front."

Thibault felt his heartbeat quicken, anticipating the moment reality bled from view. Sometimes, he thought he craved the mesh more than the Thirst itself. Sometimes.

"But—" Ors coughed, spittle slapping the interface. "Be careful up there. Tracers have been restless the last few nights, like they're waiting for something."

"Waiting for what?"

"Don't know. Whatever it is, you don't want to get between them and it. My mesh doesn't make you invisible."

Didn't he know it. The last time Thibault had encountered a tracer, he'd barely exited the slip alive. It had taken a long dive to an unpleasant stop to smash through their exit barriers, and it wasn't an experience he cared to relive, virtual or otherwise. The Trinity's security programs were dogged bastards.

"Careful. I might start to think you care."

Ors croaked out a dry chuckle. "Can't have the tracers deleting my best customer." His bulbous eyes locked on to Thibault's face. "You sure about this?"

Thibault reached over and slapped the panel before he could change his mind. The screen lit up with scrolling text.

"I'm sure," he lied.

The mesh hissed, electrodes extending. Thibault caught a hint of ozone and inhaled, savouring the sweet smell. He heard the faint squelch from hundreds of metal probes penetrating his grey matter, each aimed for a precise point. His own breathing filled his ears, and he felt his heartbeat drumming in his chest.

The mesh fought his mind to assume control, his body spasming like a discordant note at a thousand decibels. One by one, each muscle released and relaxed, synchronised signals overwhelming his subconscious.

He let go, plunging through unreality.

CHAPTER
TWO

The room warped, smearing with a mix of colours but dominated by the afterimage of blue neon. The hues swelled like a silent scream, brightening until Thibault's senses became swamped with static.

He gasped on the other side like he'd been stunned awake from a nightmare. Lightning crackled overhead, rain pelting his hair and trench coat, soaking him in seconds.

Thibault shivered. Underfoot, the solar panels of the Veeshield muted the glow of the mirrored city below. The rain smacked the dark glass in a rolling swell, filling the air with white noise.

The drops on Thibault's face made him sigh, his virtual muscles relaxing. What did it say about him that he felt more at home in the slip than in the bleed? That a reflection felt more real to him than reality itself?

A light wind rippled through his trench coat, chilling him further, though the feeling wasn't unwelcome. Huddled under the Veeshield, the city of Nova often had an oppressive, balmy heat to it, the atmosphere stale and sour. Up here, even the digital recreation of air felt fresher.

How many nights had he and Marina spent together, sitting

atop the Veeshield in the slip, watching the starlit sky? She'd always wanted to stay for the sunrise, to remember what they'd lost, but the virtual vees always made Thibault's skin feel afire.

A thumping bass drew his attention. Ors had dumped him a few hundred metres from Aurora, the open-air dawnclub perched at the highest point of the Veeshield. Thousands of revellers danced between the few sunscrapers thrusting through the enormous dome. From atop the solar plates, Nova looked like a sickly porcupine, a handful of towering spines comprising its meek defences.

Thibault shoved his hands into the pockets of his trench, advancing into the press of flesh, easing partygoers aside. Disturbed by his movements, a woman raised her head from the neck of a simulated teen, her eyes unfocused, fangs dripping with blood. Thibault flinched away from the dark pull of his Thirst, stomach clenching for a taste.

The rest of the rave was a familiar throng, fat with Trinity slaves enjoying Aurora's artificial banquet in their allotted Feast time. The sweet stench of extinct human blood assaulted Thibault's senses, a smell so pure it lodged in the back of his throat.

The skin on his neck prickled. Thibault stopped, boot heels scuffing the solar plates. A preternatural sense of being watched tickled up his spine. His gaze locked onto a figure silhouetted at the edge of the crowd. A woman, her face shadowed but familiar.

Thibault's breath stilled. It couldn't be.

She twirled and vanished, disappearing among the press.

"Stop!" Thibault screamed into the din, the word lost among the frenetic dance beats, raindrops hitting his lips.

He lurched forwards without thought, shoving aside the sweating shapes, forcing a path through. Taller than most, his gaze wove over the heads of the crowd enough to see a lone figure burst out of the gyrating mass, white hair spilling behind her like a comet's trail.

"Stop!" Thunder hammered overhead, swallowing his voice.

Thibault broke out of the crowd moments later. He spied her standing alone in the rain, hands clasped at her waist like she wasn't drenched to her skin. Lightning flashed, washing her features with stark light. His heart seized, her name falling from his lips like a whispered prayer.

"Marina."

CHAPTER
THREE

Marina tilted her head, white hair cascading over her left shoulder. She looked just as beautiful as in his neural echo, like a perfect replica.

"Mr Allard," she said in a voice not her own.

Thibault frowned, on the verge of rushing over and crushing her in a hug. Her face shimmered, exploding in brilliant light, subliming into stellar gas. The particles reformed, hardening once more into skin and hair and nightmare.

Marina disappeared, becoming someone else entirely.

"No . . ." The plea died in his throat. It wasn't possible. Not for a rider, not for someone meshed.

"My apologies for the deception." The woman's tone cut through Thibault's dismay like a frigid razor blade. Her sharp jaw held strength, mirrored in the set of her mouth and her cool regard. Close-cropped hair hugged her skull. White, like that of all vire—or at least those not vain enough to dye it. She stood poised. Ready. And impossible.

The mesh used sophisticated encryption to prevent changes to one's self-reflection at the hardware level. It wasn't possible to hack around it. Even Thibault's augmented arms reflected in the slip, his own sense of self now so acutely tied to the bionic limbs that he couldn't separate himself from them.

Which made this woman a construct. A virtual creation, like the tracers themselves, coded for a singular purpose. A program.

One that was fucking with him.

Thibault snarled, strode forwards and grabbed the construct by the throat.

"How do you know her face?" He lifted it off its feet and leaned in. "Tell me!"

It didn't fight back, didn't reach for his arm or try to pull away. It watched. Watched him choke it, with eyes so green they could have made emeralds jealous. They bored into his soul, reflecting his own snarling face. What was he doing? Strangling a construct?

Thibault swore, letting it back down and releasing his grip. "Tell me."

The look the construct returned showed no fear, and the similarity to Marina struck him, even without his wife's face. Marina's strength had captured him first, before her powerful will and unerring gift for optimism left him magnetised.

"You cannot hurt me, Mr Allard. You, or anyone else." Its feminine voice resonated deeper than he expected, threaded with roughness.

Constructs were uncommon these nights. Typically, they were created by those who operated outside the Trinity's boundaries, since the Trinity themselves had no end of servants to do their bidding.

The construct was right, though; he couldn't hurt it, not in any tangible way. But that didn't mean he had no moves.

"You'll tell me how you copied her face"—Thibault forced his fists to unclench—"or I'll summon a tracer."

That got its attention, as it was intended to. Nothing could hurt a construct—nothing except a tracer. The Trinity's digital guardians secured the slip for their masters, tracking down any unauthorised entities. Their sentence was quick, clean, and final. Deletion.

It was a bluff, of course, Thibault saying he would summon one. Accessing the slip from an unauthorised mesh could get a rider erased by a tracer just as easily. And a body without a mind was nobody at all.

In the crisp light of the construct's green eyes, Thibault saw its pupils dilate, widening into black saucers. A muscle in its neck tensed, drawing taut. Fear? From a construct?

"I need your help, Mr Allard."

"You didn't answer my question. How have you copied my wife's face? Why send me that message?"

It glanced away, then back again. "I saw you with her."

What bullshit was this? "Last chance. No more lies."

The program swallowed. "No lie, Mr Allard." It almost looked embarrassed. "I followed you into your neural echo. I saw you with her." It hesitated. "I left when I realised what it was. But I saw enough to recreate her face. I don't know where she is."

"I know you're lying." Thibault shook his head, not bothering to hide his disgust. "No one but me can enter my echo. The security protocols would have wiped you out. No construct or rider could gain access without a hundred alarms going nuclear." Ors didn't fuck around.

Steel returned to the construct's tone. "It is not a lie. I need your help."

"How am I supposed to help you?"

"I need you to find who murdered me."

CHAPTER
FOUR

Thibault stared at the construct, flashing lights from the dawnclub washing over its feminine face. Find its murderer? Someone must have hacked it somehow, made it speak nonsense. What other explanation could there be?

This had been a waste of time. Time he could have spent with Marina in his echo, feeling her soft skin, holding her close, hearing her laugh.

Except . . . how had the construct known what Marina looked like? How had it known what face to use to string him along? The question prodded him, demanding an answer.

"Where have you seen my wife before?" He held up a hand when its mouth opened. "The truth, this time."

"I'm a spectre, Mr Allard."

The idiocy of the statement was so juvenile, Thibault almost laughed. "Quit feeding me horseshit, because I ain't biting. Spectres are a damned myth, a ghost story for the gullible."

"I am no myth, as you can see."

"You're a construct. I can see that much. Why someone would code you for—"

"You asked how I knew your wife's face, how I could change my self-reflection at will, how I could enter your neural echo.

You said it yourself—what could enter it, if not a rider or construct? The answer is before you. A spectre, free of the mesh, free of controls."

A plausible explanation, but Thibault didn't buy it. He folded his arms. "If you're a spectre, prove it."

The construct frowned. "Did I not already? Taking the face of your wife?"

"Any program could do as much."

The look it gave him was baleful, and all too natural. "What program behaves as I do, Mr Allard?"

He grunted. "Thibault, kin. Not Mr Allard. If we're going to dance these steps, let's keep it simple."

The offer seemed to surprise it. As though manners mattered with the world a neon ruin.

"Very well." It inclined its head. "Thibault."

"If you're a spectre, then you've got a name."

The woman drew taller. "My name is Fortuna."

Ancient history played at the border of Thibault's memory. A goddess, wasn't she? A strange name to choose, but most vire had renamed themselves in the aftermath of the Bloodscourge, after the dust had settled and the last human had been Turned or drained dry. A futile attempt to cloak their guilt in the ashes of the past.

But Thibault Allard had kept his name, first and last. He refused to forget who he'd been, the things he'd done. Not when his memories were the only monuments.

"Say I believe you," he said. "Say I'm buying this shit. That means I'm standing here talking to a digital leftover, scraps of ones and zeroes, ready to be garbage-collected by the tracers. Why should I give a damn about a ghost?"

Fortuna's hard stare could have chilled concrete. "If you discovered all that remained of your wife was her spectre, would *she* matter?"

Thibault clenched his jaw, felt his eye twitch. Yes, Marina would matter. Always. No matter her form.

"Tell me your sob story then. Weave this tale of woe. But if it comes up short . . ." He left the threat hanging between them.

He couldn't summon the tracers on her, not really. His mesh implemented custom protocols to evade their search patterns, but they only stretched so far. Tracer malware deleted the rider and infected their exit stream, annihilating all connections. An encounter with a tracer would be as final as a bullet to the head.

The so-called spectre clasped her hands at her waist. "My husband and I were married years before the Bloodscourge, but even after we Turned, we stayed together. I stayed with him, for the memory of the man he used to be."

"Get to the point."

Fortuna pursed her mouth again, the whitening of her lips signalling the fire she kept stowed inside. How much prodding would it take to unleash it?

When she continued, steel threaded her tone. "We had a daughter, once. But she died. Leukaemia. It destroyed us, took everything, almost tore us apart. He always said the Bloodscourge stole what little remained, reforged us into something new." Fortuna shook her head. "But we weren't new. We were the same broken people as before. The hurt never left."

Thibault didn't interrupt. He understood the pain she was describing all too well.

"But unlike me," she continued, "he kept his agony contained, never let it out, never faced it. He pretended it wasn't there." Fortuna's stare probed Thibault's soul. "It festered like an open wound, putrefied him from the inside out. He took his rage out on the world, and I was always closest." She stole a raw, ragged breath, as though the words themselves had winded her.

"You're saying your husband ended you?"

"No. Finally, I . . . couldn't take it anymore. He'd become someone I didn't recognise. A demon, wearing my husband's skin. So I fled." Her delicate fingers rose to rest against her cheek. "I changed my face, escaped to the darkest corner of the city I could find. Or tried to."

"He found you?"

"No." She shook her head. "Jupiter did."

Thibault grunted. Few hadn't heard of Jupiter and his den of fanatics. A flock of dangerous fools, led by a greater one, from the stories Thibault had snatched up in passing. They called themselves the Fourth, the missing leg of the Trinity tripod, as though a middling cult could match the might of any one of the three Families. Pure hubris. Suffice to say, all Thibault had heard of the Fourth was bad news.

He scratched at his jaw. "How did you end up there?"

"With the slip, I knew he could find me anywhere, hunt me down no matter where I hid. My only chance was to change my face, make it so that not even he would recognise me. I heard of a bionics expert named Blink, who—"

"I know her." Thibault raised his chrome arms, recalling how he'd felt when he'd awoken from surgery, whole again after escaping his own thraldom. After he'd been forced to leave Marina behind. "Blink gave me these."

Fortuna nodded. "She helped me. She knew my husband. Knew his reputation. Had been forced to work for him before. That's why the Trinity leave her alone—because she does what they need, from time to time."

Thibault stared hard at her, realisation slotting into place. "Your husband is with the Trinity? What's his name?"

"Condrite."

Fuck.

Thibault sucked in a fast breath through clenched teeth. Of all the Trinity enforcers, Condrite was the worst. High in the Anuthuma ranks, any job for that blonde bastard had carved a piece from Thibault, slice by rotten slice.

"You married that slimy shit?"

Fortuna's gaze didn't waver from his face. "You know him."

"Wish I didn't."

"Then you know why I needed to get away."

"Yeah." Thibault couldn't even imagine the true depths of

Condrite's depravity. The enforcer had always taken a sick delight in seeing Thibault suffer for his work. "So what happened with Blink?"

"She did as she said she would. Broke the bones in my face, fused them back together in a different configuration, then let me stay with her while I healed."

"Must've hurt."

"That pain was my choice. That pain felt like freedom."

Freedom and pain, he understood. "What then?"

Fortuna looked down at her hands. "Jupiter's people came during the day, dressed in filthy yellow togas, crazed looks in their eyes. They took both of us."

"Blink too?" He hadn't heard anyone mention the augmenter's disappearance. Thibault owed the old vire a debt no chits could ever repay.

"They were there for Blink. Didn't know what to do with me, so they snatched me too. Jupiter wanted Blink to make him a weapon."

Thibault frowned. "Blink doesn't make weapons."

She nodded. "That's what she said to Jupiter." Her lip trembled. "He threatened me, threatened to end me if Blink didn't do as he said. So she did. Said she wouldn't have my ending staining her soul."

Sure sounded like Blink. "And then?"

"After Jupiter had what he wanted, he was going to end both of us anyway. Thought it was a great joke. So I told him who I was. Who I was married to. Who wanted me back."

Thibault could imagine Jupiter's glee when he realised the prize he had at his fingertips. The spouse of an Anuthuma enforcer at his mercy. A powerful bargaining chip.

Fortuna stared at Thibault. "I didn't do it for me, you understand? I would have preferred an ending to going back. It was my turn to help Blink."

"What did Jupiter do?"

"I told him I'd stay with the Fourth, become one of his

followers, tell him everything I knew of the Anuthuma and Condrite. But he had to let Blink go first."

Thibault hadn't heard any whispers of Blink's demise on the streets, so he could guess what had happened next. "Jupiter agreed."

Lightning flashed overhead, igniting the sky.

Fortuna nodded. "He agreed. Blink was freed, and I was not."

The low thrum of the accompanying thunder beat through his bones. "So when were you spectred?"

A pained expression passed across Fortuna's face, like the shadow of a cloud flitting over concrete. "While I was in the Feast."

That made Thibault raise an eyebrow. "The Fourth have their own meshes?"

"That's how Jupiter retains control. I think his followers stay for the Feast more than for him."

Fourth, indeed. Jupiter employed the same tactics as the Trinity themselves, offering a virtual human Feast in exchange for a price just shy of everything. How original.

Fortuna swallowed, staring at Thibault with eyes as wide as any sloid visor and shining near as bright. "I felt my brain die." If it was possible, her eyes grew wider, her lower lip trembling like she was on the verge of tears. "Like it shredded my mind, tore it apart with claws." She continued in a low whisper, barely audible, "I knew what had happened. I couldn't leave the slip, couldn't return to the bleed."

Thibault grunted. "Jupiter ended you. Case closed."

Fortuna shook her head. "No, I don't think so."

"Why not?"

"For what reason? Why would he do that?"

"He's crowned himself a god, fancies his little club as a contender to the Trinity. Sounds like he's got a few cogs missing. What more reason does there need to be?"

"You don't understand. He craves power, power over others.

It's all he wants. Before the Bloodscourge, he was someone important, I think. It eats at him, falling so low after that. You can see it in everything he does. He planned to use me against Condrite, to elevate the Fourth somehow. I don't know who spectred me, but I don't think it was Jupiter. I was too valuable to him."

"One of his followers, then."

"And risk angering their leader? The one who gifts them Feast time in exchange for their adoration? Jeopardise their only access to relief from the Thirst?"

No, she was right. It didn't make sense. The pieces didn't fit. Fortuna's story begged to be unravelled, a puzzle that tickled Thibault's curiosity. But she'd lied to him.

He hardened his tone. "I gave up my last chit for this sorry story. How do I even know you're actually a spectre? Chances are you're lying about that too."

Fortuna blinked, her brilliant irises full of an emotion that he refused to allow to touch him. "I'm telling you the truth."

He grunted. "So what happens when you try to exit now?"

"Nothing, Mr Allard. There's no connection. I can't sense my source."

"Amuse me. Try it now."

Nodding as though she'd expected him to ask, Fortuna closed her eyes. A frown webbed her forehead, but nothing else happened; she didn't vanish from the slip like a rider would when exiting.

Fortuna reopened her eyes and shrugged helplessly. Even her shrugs reminded him of Marina. Was that a genuine memory, or a fiction created by seeing her cloaked in Marina's face?

"There's nothing there. I no longer exist."

Thibault poised himself on the brink of exiting the slip, examining the thread of awareness leading back to his own source, his own body. The familiar filament disappeared when you didn't concentrate on it, like a watch on your wrist, but the moment you focused, it blazed to the forefront.

What would it be like to seek your source and not find it? Thibault shifted his trench on his shoulders, an uncomfortable heat climbing up his neck at the thought. Was she being honest with him? He had no way of knowing for sure. Ors might, he supposed, with all his slip wizardry, but Ors wasn't here.

"Say I believe you." He held up a hand to quell the hope that sprouted on her face. "And I'm not saying I do." A flicker of uncertainty. "What do you want from me? You want me to track down the Fourth, find out which of his crackpot followers ended you? Why? What's the point? If you're a spectre, then you're ended already. I can't save you like some valiant hero."

That hard line returned to her face. It was subtle: a slight tightening in her jaw, the muscles in her cheeks bulging out, round eyes tensing. But when she spoke, it was quiet, like a cool night's breeze following a blistering hot day. "I need to know. I need to know what happened to me, even if I'm not me anymore. You have to understand that. I need to know if"—she swallowed—"if *he* found me. If *he* had anything to do with it."

It took Thibault a moment to realise who she was talking about, thinking at first she was referring to Jupiter. But she meant her husband. Condrite.

"Why does that matter?"

Fortuna's posture shrank along with the volume of her voice. "Because it would mean I never got away."

Almost. She almost had him, had almost reeled him in. But not tonight. "I'm sorry, kin, I really am." He was surprised to find that he meant it. "But you lied about my wife to bring me here. I won't help you. If you truly are a spectre, and your story is as you say, then be glad you finally have your freedom, and enjoy it."

Thibault closed himself to the sudden look of hopelessness on her face. It wasn't the first time he'd inspired that look in another, and it wouldn't be the last.

Reaching for his exit, he followed the fibre back to his body, lying prone in the pod. He hit a hardened wall. Thibault froze, mental hands pushing at an enormous obstruction thrust in front of his exit. He couldn't leave. Artificial adrenaline fuelled him for flight.

Only one thing could build an exit barrier inside the slip.

He grabbed Fortuna. "You need to go! Get out of here!"

She slapped at his metal hands, a scowl painting her face. "Stop it! If you won't help, then get off me!"

Thibault growled, drawing her in. He held her face inches from his own, speaking through clenched teeth. "You don't understand. I can't exit." He leaned in close. "Tracers are here. They're here for you."

CHAPTER
FIVE

Thibault released Fortuna. Her face was stricken, panicked. "Whatever spectre tricks you've got, you better use them now," he said. "Port out of here!"

She blinked at him, eyes unfocused. "I can't."

"You snuck into my echo, didn't you?" Thibault spoke more roughly than he'd intended. "So, sneak the fuck out of here, kin!"

"I can't leave," she whispered. "The block is all around Aurora, all over the Veeshield. There's no way through."

Why did he even care? He realised that in the last few minutes, he'd crossed that jagged line between doubt and belief. He'd bought into her story like a damned fool.

Thibault swivelled on the spot, scanning their surrounds for the tracers he knew were coming. He couldn't see them. Tracers weren't subtle programs. They glowed like chilling light bulbs, declaring their presence to anyone nearby. They were designed to inspire fear; they had no need for stealth.

So where the hell were they?

He spun around once more, sure he must've missed them. The longer they stayed hidden, the more his heart raced.

Fortuna's hand grabbed his shoulder, her voice urgent. "Mr Allard."

Thibault followed her gaze upwards. Three bright, ghostly apparitions drifted down from the sunscrapers, sedate and sinister. They blazed with fiery white light, like angels descending from the heavens. Angels of death and deletion.

All three were heading straight for them. Thibault grabbed Fortuna, pulling her back towards the crowd and away from the tracers. They broke into a run, smashing through the wall of gyrating bodies and into the press.

The frenetic music crescendoed, thrumming in Thibault's veins. He shoved aside thralls and human constructs alike, not caring if he caused a disturbance. Casting a wild look over his shoulder, he snatched a glimpse of white radiance dropping below the edge of the crowd.

Someone screamed, but the speakers drowned it out, the music building to a staggered beat, rising higher and higher. Thibault and Fortuna reached the other side of Aurora right as the electronic tones shuddered to a pregnant lull. His heart stalled in concert.

A row of glowing figures lined the Veeshield beyond the crowd, hovering gently above the glass. He'd never seen so many in one place.

They were surrounded.

The beat dropped, slamming the crowd into throes of euphoria. Thibault's senses drummed with the intense bass, powerful enough that it shoved the adrenaline through his veins. Dancers flung themselves around in a maddened frenzy, everyone coated in a red sheen of blood.

"What do we do?" Fortuna screamed into his ear.

He backed away from the edge of the crowd, melting back into the throng. Revellers rammed into him from all sides, throwing themselves around in energetic moves, heedless of the tracers.

But then, thrall riders had nothing to fear. Tracers cleaned up the detritus, those who didn't belong. Spectres and constructs would be at the top of their list, and illegal riders like Thibault not far behind. They might be there for Fortuna, but he'd be wiped out all the same.

No chance. No chance at all.

Thibault hurled himself through the crowd, and she followed close behind. The mass of bodies hid the tracers from his sight, the ceaseless bass sharpening the hard edge of his fear. Sweat poured down his face, his trench coat hot and heavy around his shoulders. Strobing lights toyed with his mind, each flash an instant of despair.

People parted ahead, offering another clear view out of Aurora. Tracers drifted across the Veeshield, unhurried, closer than before. Like mannequins carved from pure light, their humanoid forms held no features: no faces, no clothes, nothing. The rain didn't touch them. Their toeless feet hung limp, hovering, casting a radiant glow on the glass below.

Glass. Below.

"There's no way out!" Fortuna's panicked cry echoed Thibault's tension.

She was right. There was no way out. Except down.

Thibault released Fortuna's hand and curled his fingers into a tight fist. He fell to one knee and hammered it downwards with every molecule of his augmented strength.

The chrome cracked the solar panel, webs of fractures exploding out from a central point. Vire yelled around him, demanding to know what he was doing, but Thibault ignored them.

He glanced at the tracers, almost upon them, then at Fortuna. "Get ready!" From the look in her eye, he could tell that she understood.

Thibault again slammed his fist into the centre of the splitting glass. It shattered on impact, imploding into a thousand shards. The entire panel disintegrated. Virtual gravity claimed him and Fortuna and the rain.

Thibault tumbled through the air, spinning end on end, the city sweeping around in long arcs, neon-lit streets growing closer on every rotation. He caught glimpses of Fortuna, falling much the same.

"Port away!" His words whipped away on the wind.

Somehow, though, she'd heard his plea. On the next pass, he saw her disappear, winking out of existence, teleporting to safety.

They'd passed beyond the block erected by the tracers. Thibault mentally scrambled for his exit, along the thread leading back to safety—and hit another barricade, solid as any steel. Still hurtling towards the city streets, Thibault realised he'd been wrong. The tracers hadn't been after Fortuna. They were after *him*.

Desperate, he dove for his exit, slamming into a brick wall within his own mind, preventing his escape. There was only one chance now. The impact wouldn't end him, not in the slip. But the violence of the collision could shove his consciousness through the tracer's barricade, smash him back into the bleed. Still, that didn't mean it wouldn't hurt.

His breath caught. His jaw seized. The ground accelerated upwards.

Thibault dove to a sudden halt. The stop happened immediately, with no sense of deceleration. One instant, he'd been hurtling down, and the next, he hovered an inch above the asphalt, so close that he could flick out his tongue for a taste.

He couldn't move, every limb bound by invisible bands. Brilliant white light swelled from all sides. He tried to scream—

And disappeared.

CHAPTER
SIX

The white light faded, bleeding from view. A hard, rocky ground was now underneath him, sulphur in the air stinking like sour eggs.

"Ah, my favourite hound! Join me, Allard, join me!"

Thibault's vision streaked with groggy colour, speckled like the vomit threatening to surge up from his stomach. Then blurred edges hardened, resolving his surrounds. Sheer rock walls rose at dangerous angles, the sheen of the slip oddly out of place. A fierce orange glow bathed the stone, pulsing gently.

Thibault rose to his knees. Then he noticed the lava. It bubbled around him in a wide circle, held at bay by the platform he knelt upon. Molten magma, mere metres away, and yet he felt no radiant heat.

A damned volcano. They were standing on a gleaming steel dais, suspended above a furnace.

"Did my pets treat you poorly, Allard?"

The voice punched Thibault in the back. It was clearer this time, and unfortunately, immediately recognisable.

Condrite.

The enforcer must have commanded the tracers to find Thibault. But why? Did the asshole know about Fortuna?

Thibault pushed himself up from the stone and brushed off his trench coat and pants. He tried to mask the dread seeping through his insides. "You didn't need to send the welcoming committee."

He saw Condrite's face first, feasting at the neck of a pale young woman, red blood soaking into her floral blouse and dripping onto the platform at their feet. Arrayed around the enforcer, several more people waited, sitting on their knees. The sight of their faces sprayed burning acid on Thibault's heart.

His marks.

Each face was one that Thibault had found for Condrite, ripped off the streets and taken to the Anuthuma in exchange for payment and a fool's hope. The hope that by working for the Trinity—for the same masters that held Marina's leash—he might discover where they had her meshed.

The five of them each stared at him, the memory of their capture seemingly as raw as the night Thibault offered them up for his own needs. So many sins, and nothing to balance the scales. Now, Condrite paraded them for Thibault in the enforcer's own Feast program, familiar faces plastered onto virtual humans.

Sick bastard.

Condrite gasped and raised his head, fangs and face coated with simulated blood. His slick, dyed hair clung to his skull, as blonde and oily in the slip as it was in the bleed. "Have a taste, Allard. They won't mind."

"Why am I here?"

The prick smirked, drawing a dainty handkerchief from the pocket of his pleated pants. He dabbed it at the corners of his mouth, then waved the bloody material. "Don't be such a bore, Allard. Have some fun! Go on, take a sip." He gestured at the kneeling woman before him. "I won't tell your parents."

Thibault didn't respond. He could see the feral gleam in Condrite's eyes and understood the sadistic pleasure the blonde vire took in tormenting him. Condrite knew that Thibault denied his Thirst, that he refused both slake and the Feast.

Condrite let out a dramatic sigh. "You're no fun, Allard." The Anuthuma enforcer glanced down. Without warning, he aimed a savage kick at the woman's ribs, his pointed black shoes cracking into her gut. "Move!"

She whimpered, but obediently slid out of Condrite's way. A beaming, blood-soaked smile returned to his face, and he tossed the handkerchief aside. It fluttered to the ground.

The woman's plight reminded Thibault of Fortuna, of the abuse she said she'd suffered at her husband's hands. He could believe it, all right. The nanofilm on his palms cried out, fingers squeezing into balled fists.

He would've liked nothing more than to smash them into that grinning face, smear it with Condrite's own black vire blood. But he couldn't. Attacking the Trinity enforcer would only mean that Condrite would get to dance in the shadows at Thibault's Dawnsdeath.

"What am I doing here?" Thibault repeated.

Condrite waggled a finger and tsked. "You're riding illegally, you naughty, naughty boy. Are you trying to make me look bad, Allard?"

Thibault kept his mouth clamped shut. This wasn't the point of their conversation. Condrite always toyed with him first, tried to get a rise, anything that he could savour later. Thibault wouldn't give him the pleasure.

The man waved his hand away. "No matter, Allard, no matter. I'll let it go this once. See how benevolent I can be?"

Thibault grunted in agreement.

"A grunt? That's it? The least you could do is thank me." A slimy smirk curled the edges of Condrite's mouth.

Thibault gave him what he wanted, if only to shorten the conversation. "Thank you."

The enforcer beamed. "That's it, Allard, that's it! Good lad. Knew you had it in you." He smoothed back his blonde hair, flattening it further against his skull, if that was possible. "I have a job for you, hound."

Thibault didn't work for the Trinity anymore—Condrite knew that. But his position was as precarious as the platform they stood upon. "What job?"

"Something a little different from your usual fare. I do so miss your company."

"Different how?"

"Have you heard of the Fourth?"

Thibault's facial muscles froze. He became aware of his posture, his hands, his body language. Could Condrite know that Thibault had been talking to Fortuna before the tracers found him?

He fought to keep his face expressionless. "Who hasn't?"

"Indeed. Jupiter and his merry band have become something of an item. But, like Icarus, the arrogant fellow has reached too far."

Condrite paused, as though expecting a response. Thibault didn't give him one. His mind was churning too much. Reached too far? Had Condrite meant Fortuna? What might the enforcer do if he knew Fortuna had come asking for Thibault's help? Would Condrite force him back into thraldom, slap on a Trinity mesh and lock him away?

"Did you know I had a wife, Allard?" The enforcer strolled over to one of the virtual women, flaring out his fingers to stroke her neck. The woman arched her back like an obedient hound, adoring gaze locked on her master. "Jupiter stole her from me, Allard. Stole her, and ended her."

Thibault controlled his breathing. In. Out. Trying to slow his racing heart, but to no avail. "I'm sorry."

"Sorry?" Condrite spun away and laughed. "Oh, Allard, you do amuse me so! Sorry, he says!" The blonde vire swooped an arm through the air. "I don't care about that fetid bitch, Allard. Jupiter *stole* from *me*, then tried to bribe me into taking her back! Can you imagine? The brass balls on this parasite!" Condrite curled both hands into fists and shook them in the air. "Must be fucking *huge!*"

"What does this have to do with me?" Thibault already had an inkling. His jangled nerves tensed. Condrite didn't care about Fortuna, didn't know that Thibault had spoken to her spectre a minute before their meeting. True to form, Condrite cared only about his bruised ego.

"Excellent question, Allard, truly incisive!" Condrite offered a gator's grin. "I want you to hunt that horrible cunt. End him for me. A little different from your usual fare, I admit, but I'm confident you can deliver."

"End him?" It was Thibault's turn to be surprised. "You don't want him brought in?"

"Oh no. Dear me, no. I don't want to mesh Jupiter. I want him gone!" Condrite clapped his hands together, then pointed a lazy finger at Thibault. "And I want my favourite hound to carry out the deed."

"I don't end folk for anyone. I'm no assassin."

Condrite sauntered over to another human, an older male with dense white hair and a curled fringe. Thibault couldn't even remember his name.

The enforcer wove around behind the adoring figure. His hand snaked out and snagged a fistful of white locks, wrenching back. The captive's adoring gaze never wavered.

"No assassin, Allard?" The mirth vanished from his eyes. "You remember this one? You do, don't you? He owed me, Allard. Filthy slaker, too poor to pay his debts. And do you know what he did after you brought him to me, after I offered him a cosy mesh and a life in the slip to repay his debt? He spat at me, Allard. At me! Can you believe it?" Condrite traced a finger along the man's neck. "I took his head instead. But not before I tore off his limp dick and sagging balls and crammed them down his throat."

Condrite wiped his hand on his pants, then strolled to another woman. He stopped in front of her, hands on his hips.

Thibault remembered her name. Angela. He'd seen it on her readout before he stole her from an Isos terminus and delivered her to Condrite, the only time the enforcer had tasked him with taking a thrall from one of the other Trinity.

"And you remember her too, Allard? Or is your memory failing? This traitorous thrall thought she could flee to Isos, those yellow bastards." Half turning, Condrite smiled at Thibault. "I don't abide traitors, Allard. And I don't do second chances." He cupped his hand around the woman's neck. "I strangled her with a mesh cord until she passed out, then shot her in the head."

The enforcer continued, turning to fully face Thibault now. "So you see, Allard, you're already a murderer. You're already my assassin. You think the fools you bring to me lead happy, full lives once you hand them over? Are you truly so delusional?"

Thibault felt a rising heat soak his face, radiating up from his pounding heart. Condrite had ended all of them.

He looked from face to face, recalling each one, each payment. An ending had never been the bargain. Thraldom, yes. That was bad enough. But not murder.

The whole time though, he'd never been under the illusion that he could control what Condrite did with his marks after he handed them over. It wasn't Thibault's responsibility . . . was it?

"Your shock is exquisite, Allard, truly exquisite!" Condrite threw back his head and laughed, harsh and mocking.

Thibault clenched his jaw to keep a foul curse from lurching out. He was no murderer. "Find someone else. This job isn't for me."

"No?" The mirth died on Condrite's face, vanishing in an instant. "You refuse?" The enforcer's voice dropped, low and quiet. He pointed to the virtual humans. "Do you know what the difference is between you and them?"

Thibault didn't reply.

"Nothing." Condrite made a cutting motion with his hand. "No fucking difference at all. I say the word, and the great thrallhound Thibault Allard becomes the hunted himself. You think you can escape my mesh once I decide you should wear it for your crown? You'll do as I fucking say." His voice rose to a shout, spit flying from his lips. *"As I fucking say!"*

The woman at Condrite's feet moaned, her head drawn back, the enforcer's hand clutching a fistful of her hair, squeezing so tight it lifted her eyebrows. He kneeled down, bringing her face close to his, then sneered up at Thibault.

"I thought you were better trained than this." The enforcer's voice seethed with sibilance. "You will find Jupiter, and you will end him . . ." His tongue flicked out, tasting the woman's cheek, sliding to her forehead. "Else I will find new amusement with your wife."

Thibault's guts vaulted over his rib cage. Condrite knew? Knew who he'd been searching for?

Condrite smirked. "Marina, isn't it?"

"You have her?" The question fled before Thibault could hold it back.

"I know where she is, Allard." He traced his index finger along the path of his saliva. "The question is . . . how much do you care?"

"Tell me. Tell me where she is." He hated the begging tone he heard in his own voice.

"Perhaps." Condrite rose, staring down his nose. "Deliver Jupiter's heart, and perhaps I will return yours."

Thibault struggled to breathe, the air refusing to soak into his lungs. What if Condrite was lying? Could he take that chance? The answer was obvious.

He and Marina had gone willingly to their thraldom with the Anuthuma. Though it was possible they'd traded her to Ortrea or Isos, the likelihood was that she remained in an Anuthuma terminus. He couldn't afford to say no.

"Where can I find him?" Thibault's tone came out like a choked growl.

"Capitulating so soon, Allard?" Condrite pouted like a child. "I'm disappointed!"

"Tell me where to find him, and I'll do what needs doing." The words tasted like refuse on his tongue.

Condrite grinned. "You're the hound, aren't you, Allard? So . . . sniff him out! I don't know where to find the fool. In some hole, no doubt. Return to me when the deed is done, and I will have your usual fee, plus a little extra."

"You'll tell me where to find her."

"Demands, Allard?" Condrite raised an eyebrow.

"Promise me."

"Promise?" The enforcer's grin widened, showing his fangs. "I promise you one thing, Allard. I promise that when your task is done, you will have no more need for hope." He turned his head back to the woman kneeling on the steel ground. "Now, my dear . . . where were we?"

Thibault bunched his hands into tight fists and took a step forwards. "I want—"

Condrite flung his hand out in a dismissive wave, then dove for the woman's neck.

Tight bands grasped Thibault around his middle, thrusting him backwards. Darkness rushed to fill the edges of his vision. The volcano scene shrank to a pinpoint and vanished.

CHAPTER
SEVEN

Thibault exploded through his exit, his consciousness blasted out of the slip. Azure light blundered into view, sweeping aside the prevailing darkness. Shining tubes invaded his sight, stinging his eyes, making him blink against the glare. He heard a faint, slick squelch from the mesh atop his head—the electrodes leaving his brain tissue. The ports dotting his scalp vibrated and closed.

He groaned, his real muscles rebelling against his desire for movement, a sharp contrast to the virtual ones of the slip. Sliding the mesh from his head, he massaged his stubbled jaw. Somehow, Condrite had evicted him from the slip. Thibault had been lucky to get out with his mind intact.

"I can see from that thundercloud you didn't find what you expected." Ors' rasping tones cut through the fog of Thibault's transition.

"You read right." Thibault's throat was so dry, he felt like he'd been scorched himself. He swung his legs off the slip pod and stood, swaying a little.

"Easy. That was a long ride. Give it time."

Time. Right. He had all the time he could ever need, but it was never enough.

"How did it go?" Ors leaned on the armrest of his recliner, the cracked blue leather creaking a complaint in return. "So, who sent that message?"

"What do you know of the Fourth?"

"The fourth what?"

"Jupiter's Fourth."

"Oh, *that* Fourth."

"You know much about it?"

Ors cleared his throat. A glob of mucus fled from his melted lips, lurching out onto the carpet. Thibault paid it no mind. With Ors, you got used to these things.

The scarred vire's face took on a thoughtful expression—or at least, that was how Thibault interpreted it based on Ors' few surviving facial muscles.

"Don't know much, though more than I'd care to. Jupiter fancies himself a new age god, hence the colourful name. Those that seek him out have a tendency to disappear, lost to whatever fiction he's concocted for them." Ors shrugged, their fate of no consequence to him. "What does he have to do with Marina?"

"Nothing. And everything."

"You might need to explain that one to me."

"Any idea where to find the Fourth?"

Ors peered at Thibault, a hint of skin tightening around his bulbous eyes. It had taken Thibault a long time to bear such scrutiny from Ors. With the eyelids and surrounding tissue liquified, those eyes protruded from their sockets in a way that reminded Thibault of the old cartoons. But the desolation in Ors' expression was where comedy came to die.

"You know the rules of this game. Tit for tat." The vire extended a bony finger and tapped it on the desk three times. "Pay the piper, then we can start shit-shooting."

Thibault felt his mouth curl at the wry humour. He set his last chit onto the desk. "Reckon you might have that ass backwards."

Ors choked out a dry chuckle, sandpaper on steel. "So what do you want with the Fourth?"

"You wouldn't believe me if I told you."

The vire's bald head cocked to one side, the welded skin on the other stretching dangerously. Thibault tried not to notice.

"Now you got me curious," Ors said.

Thibault leaned against the desk. He crossed one leg over the other, then crossed his arms for good measure. He looked at the tattered carpet, more filth and grime now than synthetic fibres.

"There was a reason you couldn't trace the message. It came from a spectre." Noticing Ors lean forwards in his peripheral vision, he waited a moment for the mockery, but it never came. He continued. "Said she'd been taken by the Fourth. Ended sometime after, with the mesh still on her head, but didn't know how, or who."

"And this spectre wanted you to find out."

Thibault raised his head and met Ors' eyes, expecting to see them shining with mirth. Instead, the blue irises were serious, levelled at him like smoking gun barrels.

"You believe me?"

"Why wouldn't I? Never known you to be a fool."

Thibault studied Ors. "You ever meet one before? A spectre?"

Ors nodded, eyes gleaming. "They're rare. You get unpredictable results ripping a mind from the slip, ending or otherwise. But it can happen."

"How? I thought spectres were a myth. A ghost story."

Ors shrugged. "It's not so unbelievable. The mesh translates your sense of self into digital form, converts your consciousness into code and links it back to your mind. If the link is severed in the right way, the program persists. Separate, but whole."

It made an odd sort of sense. Strange to think he could be disconnected from himself in the slip, spend his nights locked out of his body. Thibault shivered, an imagined draught of icy wind brushing the back of his neck.

"So Jupiter ended her? Or one of his lackeys?" Ors asked.

Thibault shook his head. "Don't know."

Ors went silent for a moment, that implacable gaze fixed on Thibault's face. "And Marina? This spectre knows where to find her? That why you're helping her?"

"I didn't say I was helping her, only that I met her. She said she went to the Fourth to escape her husband. And guess who that is."

"Who?"

"Condrite."

Ors grunted. "Hard to believe someone would marry that piece of shit."

"There's more. Right after I heard her sob story, Condrite's tracers nabbed me, pulled me into his Feast. He had another job for me."

"You should never have got involved with the Trinity."

It wasn't the first time Ors had scolded Thibault, so he didn't argue the point. They both knew why he'd done it. Hunting their thralls meant discovering their termini, slow and arduous as the process was. And in one of those termini was Marina. Only a matter of time, he'd thought. What a fool he'd been.

Thibault didn't mention the faces he'd seen in Condrite's Feast program, or what Condrite had told him about their fates.

Ors sighed, shaking his head. "What does the blonde prick want?"

"Wants me to end Jupiter."

"End him? Why now? Jupiter's been nursing his crappy cult for years."

"Condrite says Jupiter murdered Fortuna."

Ors coughed, barking rasps that sounded like he might choke to death. Thibault had known him long enough to know that the burned vire wasn't in any danger. No. He was laughing.

"So, one mystery solved," Ors managed between breaths. "And another noose tied. What will you do?"

Thibault looked down at his hands. The scuffed chrome appeared burnished with blue under Ors' neon lights. "I'll find

Jupiter. I have no choice. Condrite knows about Marina. Says he knows where she is."

"Shit." Ors' laughter died away, and his tone deepened. "I'm sorry."

Thibault raised his head. "What else do you know about Jupiter? Fortuna said he was someone important before the Bloodscourge."

Ors chuckled. "Way I heard it, he was rolling in money, right up there in high society. A billionaire, they say. But then the Bloodscourge came, and all that money couldn't buy the one thing we all craved." He shook his head. "An ego to match Everest, and impotent as a eunuch. A volatile combination."

Sounded like one hell of a chip on Jupiter's shoulder.

"Know where I can find him?"

Ors responded without hesitation. "In a Barren. No doubt about that. But which one? They say the only way to find the Fourth is to first lose yourself."

Thibault turned to go. "Shouldn't be hard, then." A Barren made sense. If Jupiter kept his cult hidden from the Trinity, he had to go somewhere invisible to the slip.

Ors wasn't finished. "And what about Fortuna?"

Thibault stopped at the door, hand on the doorframe, and glanced back. "What about her?"

Ors swivelled his armchair away, shaking his head. "Just don't get yourself ended, Tibs. You're my best customer."

"You can count on it, kin."

Thibault strode through the blue-lit corridor and out into the street, closing the heavy steel door behind him.

Time to track down a god.

CHAPTER
EIGHT

Thibault wasn't sure what kind of reception he'd receive at Blink's, but she was the only thread he had to tug on. He walked the seven blocks to her salvage yard, past streets he could remember strolling down with Marina by his side. In his memories, they held hands as they walked, the sun making her hair a lighter shade of brown.

Fragments and images intruded on his thoughts, brief flashes he couldn't be sure were real. He wondered which pieces his imagination had supplied to balance the erosion. It came as a relief when he finally arrived at Blink's depot, the holographic sign out front bold in its simplicity: *[Scrap]*.

Cracked, lifeless visors peeked out from a mass of discarded sloid parts and other junk, each regarding Thibault in mute judgement. The piles of scrap were higher than the last time he'd been there, and more varied in their composition.

The ambient light of the city struggled to invade the haphazard laneways of stacked detritus, sharp angles casting jagged shadows. Dirt crunched under Thibault's boots, dark patches of black oil soaked in other misshapen sections.

It had been decades since he'd last been here. Then, Thibault had barely comprehended the surrounds, his gaping shoulder sockets leaking a steady stream of black blood and strength. He'd been too focused on staying upright and conscious to notice anything else.

The corrugated metal shack came into view around one of the scrap piles, lit from within by a warm orange glow. A squat thing, floating in a sea of discarded technology, like a tiny hut buried by a metallic mountain range.

Thibault patted his reaver, holstered underneath his trench, the slake injectors he kept in the pocket tinkling against each other. He wasn't sure what reception he'd receive from Blink, but if it was an unwelcome one, he wanted to be ready.

He stopped in front of the rusty iron door and beat his fist against it three times.

Clang! Clang! Clang!

Thibault heard shuffling. A muttered curse.

The door swung open, old hinges screaming for lubrication. Blink's shining augmented eyes appeared, a radiant blue at first, then transitioning through forest green and orange. She stood a full foot shorter than him, but the physical difference didn't stop her from making him feel small. Her hair hung lank against her neck, a greasy off-white, desperate for a hint of soap.

She made no move to invite him inside. "You shouldn't have come back here." Blink's voice held the same gravelly monotone he remembered.

"I need your help, kin."

Her unerring optical discs flickered to violet, then scarlet, then back again. "That so."

"I met a spec—"

"Toss the blunderbuss behind you."

Thibault paused, mouth still open from being cut off. No doubt she'd picked out the weapon with one of her vision enhancements.

He didn't reach for the gun. "I ain't here for you. Just need your help is all."

The door hinges squealed again, the corrugated iron

swinging shut. Thibault stopped it with a metal hand, making it clang.

Blink's eyes squalled to black, twin voids boring into his skull. The air crackled with charge, ready to be released.

Thibault quickly held up his other hand, palm out, facing her. "All right, kin! All right, you win. Go easy."

Reaching into his trench, he eased his reaver free of its leather holster, thumb and forefinger clasping the metal stock. Blink's gaze didn't waver from his face, not when the weapon crossed between them or when he flicked it over his shoulder. It clattered into the dirt.

Blink's eyes glowed silver, and she swivelled away from the door, allowing Thibault to let himself in. He followed behind, scanning the room, searching for any of her tricks. The door banged shut in his wake. The sour smell of the city turned musty, like a dishcloth in need of detergent.

A mixture of soft frequencies permeated the room, whirring, rumbling, clicking, clacking. Everywhere Thibault looked, something metal moved. A brass gear cycled on a motor, spinning on its own. Nearby, a pair of pistons hammered, faint hisses accompanying each thrust. Wiring littered another surface, a range of colours and thicknesses, waiting for connection.

The shack seethed with technology, all of Blink's projects on display in different states of disarray. In the corner stood a gurney, topped by a thin layer of cushioning long since deflated, the faux leather stained with dried patches of black vire blood.

Thibault remembered lying on top of it, weary with pain, longing for it to stop. He recalled Blink leaning over him, her incandescent eyes the last thing he saw before the sedatives swallowed his mind. When he'd awoken, he had new arms. The same ones he bore now.

Thibault's gaze tracked Blink's retreat into the shack. She stopped by a desk, rummaging around the stack of paraphernalia littered on top.

"Like I said." Thibault rubbed his jaw. "I need your help—or at least, someone else does."

"Time enough for that." Blink swung around, her eyes that warm, reflective orange once again.

He frowned, staring at her. It was bright enough that he could see his own mirror image in her eyes, his long, unkempt white hair framing a drawn, weathered face.

Something moved in the reflection, deep inside. Too late, he realised that it wasn't part of Blink's eyes. It was something behind him. Metal clamped down on each of his forearms, matte-grey fingers stronger than steel. His arms signalled pain, but Thibault locked it down, ignored it.

Blink had deliberately distracted him when he entered, led him away from the door so he wouldn't see what waited behind it. A sloid. A damned, clanking sloid.

"What is this?" Thibault didn't bother to mask the anger in his tone. "Call off your dog, or I'll add it to your junk pile."

"I am no canine, sir," an electronic voice buzzed next to Thibault's ear. "And there shall be no violence within the abode of my Madam."

Blink clicked her tongue, flicking the moist flesh at her teeth like she was trying to dislodge a hunk of meat. It was only then that he noticed what she'd picked up from the table. A sparkling clean, jaw-toothed surgical saw.

Burnished yellow replaced the reflective orange as Blink replied, "Thank you for returning what's mine."

"No violence in this abode," the sloid's warble hummed again. "Unless, of course, Madam wishes it."

CHAPTER
NINE

The sloid wrenched Thibault's arms out to the sides, spread-eagling him on the spot. Thibault strained, expecting the power in his augmented limbs to overcome the sloid's strength with ease.

Nothing happened. He hung helpless, feet barely touching the hardwood floor of the shack. Blink stalked towards him, balancing the gleaming scalpel between her thumb and forefinger, a squat reaper of retribution. Her gaze flowed from his left shoulder to his right, examining them, probably deciding which to cut.

"What the hell is this?" Thibault infected his voice with all the rage he could muster, despite the quavering fear coiled around his guts. His mind flashed with images of stumbling through the city streets, shoulder sockets on fire, bloodied and weak.

Blink paused in front of him, glancing up as though she'd forgotten he was there, so focused on the surgery she was planning. Blue, green, red, yellow again. Her eyes danced a rainbow of promised pain.

"I gifted you those arms out of pity, boy. It impressed me, you escaping the Anuthuma terminus. It took strength.

Determination. Precious few do what you did, boy, precious few." Blink's mouth twisted into a rictus snarl, her voice as sharp-edged as the scalpel she wielded. "And what did you do with my gifts?" Her tone went whisper-quiet, low, laced with threat. "You used them to round up poor souls for the Trinity. My arms. You used *my arms*. You . . . you . . . you . . ." Blink shook her head. "I don't have a word for you. The word to describe you hasn't been invented yet." She raised the saw. "But I'll be taking back what's mine, boy. You can be sure of that."

"Wait." Thibault strained against the implacable grip of the sloid. "You don't understand!"

"I understand. More than you know."

Thibault tried to suck in a breath, lungs pulled taut, but the air refused to obey. "I had to do it." He wheezed, lights dancing in his eyes from the lack of oxygen. "I need to find my wife. The Trinity are the only ones who know where she is. I had to do their dirty work."

Blink stared up at him, blurred features unreadable down the bridge of his nose, too close to see her clearly. "Is that supposed to convince me? How many have you given to the slip for your need, boy? How many?"

Too many. The thought sheared its way into his mind, slicing through his rationalisations. Far too many. He couldn't say that to Blink, though. Could barely admit it to himself.

He said the only thing that sprang to mind in his defence. "I love her."

"Love." Blink sounded like she'd tasted something foul, something that made her want to retch. "To claim love for what you do . . ."

She growled then, a deep rumble at the back of her throat, the sound wolves used to make before they dove for your jugular. "And what would this love of yours think if she knew? What happens if you free her, and she learns what it took? What then?"

Thibault flinched. He tried to force away the sudden image of Marina watching him as he told her what he'd done.

"She'd hate it. Maybe hate me too." The words tumbled out in short breaths. "But she'd be free."

Blink didn't respond for a long moment, standing so close to his hanging body, all he could see was the top of her head. He expected to feel the jagged bite of the saw at his shoulder, separating the grafts bonding metal to flesh, but no pain came. Not yet, at least.

"You know enough to know that, I see." Blink's head bobbed away from him, and she threw up her hands. "Faugh! Put him down, Reggie. Nothing I do to him is going to compare with what he's doing to himself."

"Your pleasure, Madam." The sloid's arms dropped, slamming Thibault back to the ground, jarring his knees. Still, the thing didn't let go, keeping a powerful grip on his forearms.

Thibault heaved in a gasp. He hadn't realised until then how much the arms meant to him, how much they made him whole.

Blink tossed the scalpel onto a bench, where it clattered against the other metal. "If you want help tracking another poor soul, boy, you've come to the wrong place."

Thibault shook his head, white hair swaying in front of his face. "This is something different."

"Spit it out then, and begone. You're fouling up the place."

Thibault tried to glance over his shoulder and get a look at the sloid, this "Reggie," but he only caught a snatch of silver in his peripheral vision.

"You can hardly talk, using a thrall to do your dirty work."

"A thrall? Psssht! My Reggie's no thrall. He's pure metal and electrons, though he's still got more heart than you."

"But it's a sloid. Who's the pilot?"

"I am no simple *sloid*, sir." Reggie inflected the word like it tasted revolting.

Blink blinked at Thibault, or at least gave the closest thing to a blink she could with her metallic discs: they flashed from teal to green, then back again. "You think a sloid needs a vire mind in the rider's seat? Sloids are nothing more than shells for commands, avatars to roam the bleed. Doesn't matter where those commands originate. I programmed Reggie myself. A simple construct, to be sure, but he doesn't come with all the baggage of a Thirst-ridden mind."

"Indeed, I carry baggage too, when required." Reggie sounded proud of that fact.

"Can he let me go?"

Blink's eyes darkened a few shades to a pulsing aqua, and her mouth split into a feral grin. Her teeth sparkled with the burnished hue of quicksilver, every tooth replaced by a metal Thibault couldn't identify. "You don't get to use those arms in my place. My Reggie'll crush you to pulp before you take me in."

Reggie's voice buzzed again. "The key to a good pulping is in the elbows. Most believe wrist action is the most important, but only the elbow can achieve the torque necessary to splinter bone."

Thibaut tried not to think about how Reggie had worked that out. He spoke to Blink instead. "I don't want to take you anywhere. I'm here for your help."

"You said that already. Repeating it doesn't make me believe you. Say your piece and get out."

Thibault sighed, accepting the restraints on his arms. He couldn't blame her, not really. He wouldn't trust himself, either.

"I'm here to help someone you worked on. A woman. She escaped from . . . a rough life."

Blink's eyes flashed pink. "You'll have to give me more than that. This woman have a name?"

"Fortuna."

She stiffened, her eyes plunging to black. "You've uttered the wrong name. I know what it's like to live as she did, and I'll accept my own end before I'm party to that." Blink flicked out her hand. "Reggie! You know what we do with garbage."

"Wait!" Thibault struggled to no avail. "Dammit, Blink! Wa —"

Reggie spun Thibault in an arc like a rag doll. "Is it pulping time, Madam?" The sloid's foot clanged into the iron door, swinging it open. The junkyard waited outside, shadowed and dark.

Blink's voice rose behind Thibault. "No, Reggie. But give him a taste of the mud, would you?"

"Certainly, Madam. My pleasure."

Reggie wrenched Thibault's arms behind him, then drew him back so far he thought the sloid meant to toss him further inside. But he flew forwards instead, wheeling through space, out into the yard.

Thibault slammed into wet mud, shoulder first, and slid to a stop. White fire burned his shoulder, but that was the least of his worries. He craned his neck towards the lit doorway, sighting Reggie's blurred silhouette clomping towards him. The sloid comprised a haphazard set of mismatched parts, no colours of the Trinity in evidence, all the paint removed until its chassis shone in silver.

Thibault sought his reaver. His only chance. It lay in the mud two metres away. But he barely had time to register his impotence. The sky above him darkened, moonlight snapped off. The sloid's rubber-soled heel hovered over his face.

"Don't come back here again, boy," Blink's voice came from the shack. "If you do, you'll regret it."

The foot flashed down. Then there was only the void and the acrid flavour of mud.

CHAPTER
TEN

A blinding flash of green made Thibault squint. His head hurt all over, an aching throb like his skull was expanding and contracting with every heartbeat. The scent of earth filled his nostrils, dirt and mud and decay.

His face wouldn't move. It felt stuck fast, like someone had glued it shut. A small groan escaped his lips. He hawked and spat, his mouth full of grit. Flakes of dried mud followed the gob to the pavement.

Thibault pushed himself into a sitting position. His head spun, and the world lurched. He paused, hand to head, waiting for the feeling to pass.

A frown sent more dried muck dropping into his lap. He brushed a hand over his face, rubbing his eyes, mouth and nose. Mud caked his hair, and he did his best to dislodge it, but his fingers kept catching on his slip plugs, sending spikes of lightning into his brain.

That sloid had packed a punch. Or a kick. Whatever—it hurt.

Thibault glanced up. The source of the green light hung overhead, Blink's hologram pronouncing simply: [Scrap].

They'd dragged him back to the street in front of the junkyard and dumped him. Could've been worse. Blink had left his arms, at least, and his reaver lay nearby. Thibault had no idea how long he'd been out. Long enough for them to drag him to the street and for the mud to dry, at least.

He had to go back. Blink knew more about Jupiter, that much was clear. One way or another, he needed to make her talk.

How?

Fortuna. For whatever reason, Blink gave a damn about the woman.

Thibault hauled himself to his feet, head pounding like an old washing machine. He fetched his reaver and holstered it, then staggered back into the junkyard, weaving his way through the piles, considering what he'd yell through the door.

As it turned out, he didn't need to. He stumbled upon Blink and Reggie out in the yard, the aged mechanic rummaging through a pile of parts, mumbling something to herself. Her eyes glowed bright gold, lighting up the space before her.

Reggie saw Thibault first, the silver sloid swinging his head without moving the rest of his body. "Madam, I believe regrets are required."

Blink didn't turn around. "What's that, Reggie?"

"The errant boy has returned. Your last instructions were that if he reappeared, regrets would ensue."

Now Blink did move. She straightened from her crouch, clutching a piece of plating. It looked like an upper arm shell coated in Ortrea blue, but Thibault was no engineer.

He held up his hands, palms out. "Hold up there, Elbow Grease. Just gotta talk. That's all, hear?"

"Shall I pulp him now, Madam?" Reggie flexed his right arm. "My elbow is functioning magnificently."

Blink's eyes darkened to a black so complete, it seemed Thibault could see the night through her skull. She opened her mouth.

Thibault didn't wait for whatever she had planned. "Fortuna's a spectre! A damned spectre! Someone already ended her. I'm trying to help, find out who did it, give her some peace. You get it? I'm on her side!"

"A spectre?" Blink asked in a quiet voice. "Explain yourself."

"She came to me in the slip, asked for my help, said she was murdered while meshed. Spectred. She wants me to find who did it, kin. You're my only lead."

Blink cocked her head to the left. "And you agreed to help her?"

Thibault considered his options. He could lie, tell Blink this was all about helping Fortuna . . . but who knew what those bionics could see? Perhaps they could even spot a lie. "No, I didn't agree."

Lime-coloured eyes darkened to forest green. Thibault stepped forwards before Blink could respond. "Condrite's tracers nabbed me, took me to him. He had another job for me."

"What job?"

"Jupiter." Thibault paused, sure he caught a glimmer of recognition. "He wants Jupiter ended for murdering his wife."

Blink snorted. "His pride hurt, was it? That blonde bastard never cared about anyone but himself."

"That's about the measure of it."

"And you agreed to be his killer?"

"Don't have a choice."

"You always have a choice, even when they're all shitty."

"I chose the least shitty." He paused. "But perhaps I can give Fortuna's spectre some peace too."

Blink's expression was unreadable. "And you've come to me to find out where Jupiter is skulking?"

Thibault nodded. "Fortuna told me his goons took the pair of you after you helped her."

"Did she also tell you what happened when we got there?"

"You made him something. A weapon. She traded her life for yours."

"Bah! You've got zero chance, boy. I already hired someone to fetch her out of there, someone a lot more capable than you. He's been gone long enough now he ain't coming back." She waggled a finger in his direction. "And neither will you."

"Let me worry about me."

Blink scoffed, her mercury-coloured fangs glinting for an instant. "I don't intend to worry at all, you can be sure of that. Now sod off, or my Reggie will juice you like a lemon."

Reggie held up his right arm, twisting his forearm at the elbow. "As they say, to murder is human. To juice . . . is divine!"

Blink glanced at the sloid. "No one says that, Reggie."

The sloid appeared unperturbed by the statement, his elbow emitting a faint click on each rotation.

Thibault eyed the oscillating appendage. "What does it cost you to help me?"

The old vire reached up to scratch her cheek, those unsettling eyes disassembling his soul. "How did this spectre know she'd been ended? Doesn't require an ending to create one, so they say. Could've been disconnected." Blink flared her fingers. "Mesh ripped free."

"She was convinced, that's all I know."

"And how do you know it was actually Fortuna? What if this is some ploy by Condrite to get her back? Could've created a construct to fool you."

Thibault stared at Blink. He hadn't considered that Condrite himself could have sent Fortuna. Still, he shook his head. "No . . . I don't think so."

"Why not?"

For a moment, he searched for the words. "I believed her. Truth has a ring to it."

Blink scoffed again. "Adept lies ring too."

"Maybe so. But the only way to find out is to find Jupiter's hiding place."

"Olympus."

Thibault frowned. "What?"

Blink sniffed and rubbed the back of her hand across her

nostrils. "Olympus, boy. That's where you can find Jupiter. That's what he calls his demented den."

"So you know where it is?"

She pursed her lips. "More or less."

"More or less?"

"I can show you the way in. But I don't think you'll be coming back out. You want suicide-by-fanatics? So be it."

Thibault held his breath, not daring to speak now that Blink was close to telling him how to find this Olympus.

She tapped a metal eye with her fingernail. "Jupiter's cronies ripped these from my head before they took us. Easier, I suppose, than using a blindfold." She smiled. "They didn't want us to know where we were going. Didn't know what I could see, so they stole the doubt away. Or so they thought."

Blink thrust the same bony finger into her eardrum and wiggled it around. "They forgot that the blind have to see without eyes, that we have other senses to make up the difference."

Extracting the finger, she flicked whatever she'd found to the dirt. "Reggie."

Reggie's arm finally stopped moving, and the sloid strode forwards until he was by Blink's side. "What do you desire, Madam? A wrench? A spigot? A neck massage?"

Neck massage?

"Take this fool to where you took Tyre, in the undercity, you remember?"

"My memory banks are functioning to spec, Madam."

"Good. Take the hunter there and replay the same instructions."

"Certainly!" Reggie clomped forward, arms swinging. He passed by Thibault, waving a hand through the air. "Come, Sir Fool! A journey is afoot!"

Thibault nodded his thanks at Blink and turned to go.

"Boy." Her voice made him pause and glance back. Her eyes

shone like white diamonds. "If you find she's still with Jupiter . . . that she's alive . . . you bring her out, you hear?"

Thibault nodded. "I hear you, kin."

"You better, boy. You better."

He swung away, following the departing sloid out of the junkyard.

CHAPTER
ELEVEN

The shining sloid set a frenetic pace through the streets of Nova, faster than Thibault could comfortably walk without the occasional jog. He wondered if Blink had configured that speed deliberately, to make the trek as uncomfortable as possible.

Reggie strode like a power walker, arms pumping back and forth, bent at perfect right angles. The pistons driving his legs hissed and gasped with each stride, rubber soles scuffing the concrete.

They passed a trio of golden Isos sloids gathered around the entrance to a work site, gesturing animatedly to each other. The discussion choked off when Reggie neared, and three backlit yellow visors locked on the approaching silver robot.

Thibault couldn't blame them. Sloids came in the three colours of the Trinity these nights: red, blue, or yellow. Spying a silver one was like spotting a human roaming the streets. Well, maybe not that strange.

Reggie tipped an imaginary bowler hat at the Isos sloids. "Make way, ladies and gentlemen, make way! There's a good thrall!"

Two of the metal figures moved aside, probably too surprised to do anything else, but the third planted itself directly in

Reggie's path. Its visor swelled, a spotlight beaming onto Reggie and Thibault.

Thibault raised one hand against the harsh glare, the other dipping into his trench coat, ready to tug his reaver free if the pilot caused trouble. Thibault couldn't injure the thrall; the pilot was meshed in a terminus somewhere, operating the sloid from the slip. But he could probably incapacitate the avatar's frame with a few well-aimed shells.

In the end, he didn't need to worry. Reggie never broke stride, powering towards the yellow sloid. "Pardon, good sir! We have need of this pathway!"

The sloid crossed its arms. "What in the Progenitor's name are you then, eh?"

"No time for chitchat!" Reggie approached, grasped the sloid's neck plate with his left hand, leaned down in the same motion and hooked his other hand behind the sloid's knee joints.

"What the blaz—"

Reggie flipped the flailing figure like it weighed no more than a bag of cloth, its legs arcing up and over its head. It dropped to the pavement on its front with a clanking crash. The thing scrabbled at the concrete, muffled swearing emerging from damaged speakers.

Thibault gave the other sloids an apologetic shrug and jogged after Reggie. He'd have to remember not to piss him off. "So where are we going, kin?"

"The undercity, sir."

"Which part of the undercity? Kind of a big place."

"An abandoned sector, sir."

Abandoned? Thibault stopped himself from reaching inside his trench for his reaver again.

The undercity had originally been a subway network back in the old world. After the Bloodscourge, the surviving vire had sought refuge from the vees, converting the subway into an underground city. Then the Trinity built the Veeshield, and the undercity became largely abandoned, barring a few secured sectors. Now, skinners roamed the empty places, searching for an easy meal. Jupiter was bold to have carved out a hideaway there, but it explained why no one knew where he dwelled.

Thibault glanced at the sloid. If skinners found them, they wouldn't be interested in Reggie, and he wasn't sure the sloid would help keep the fleshmad at bay.

"And so we descend into the depths, sir!" Reggie made a sharp right turn at the next corner, striding to a decrepit subway entrance. Stairs descended into a gaping maw of darkness.

The undercity breathed violet vapour, steam from its belly rising into the night air, catching the light cast from a shining billboard overhead.

"You don't need to call me sir, Reggie. I'm no gentleman."

"Certainly, sir! How shall I refer to you in the future?"

They took the first steps into the undercity, the echoes of their steps growing louder as they descended into the murk. Thibault frowned down the stairs and muttered under his breath, "How about 'damned fool'?"

"As you wish, Damned Fool! Though I must say, it doesn't have quite the same connotation of respect."

Twin beams of light shone forwards from Reggie's helmet, a pair of headlamps Thibault hadn't noticed earlier brightening into life.

Thibault sighed. "Just call me sir, kin."

"Very well, Sir Kin."

Thibault rolled his eyes. Reggie's headlamps prevented the need for Thibault's night vision to take over, though he wondered if he wouldn't have preferred that. The lights cast stark shadows, splitting the darkness through the centre, lending an eerie weight to the view.

"Just sir, Reggie. That's all. Sir."

"Aha! I see, sir!" Reggie emitted a static chuckle. "You have a penchant for wit, sir, yes indeed!" They reached the bottom of the stairwell on the final syllable, and Reggie's warbling tones echoed back from the wide undercity corridor. Abandoned shops lined either side, two rows of pillars throwing long shadows.

"Turn your volume down," Thibault said in a low voice. "We don't want to attract unwanted attention. Skinners roam these parts."

"Understood, sir." Reggie's reply was a soft murmur. "Never fear, sir. I am easily replaced should the fleshmad decide to dismantle me. The Madam builds more and more, even as we speak! Soon I will have a great many friends with which to conversate." Reggie paused. "Though I should say, sir, I believe you are in more danger from the fleshmad than I, for I am fleshless." He held up one of his arms. "See, sir? One hundred percent flesh free!"

Reggie's voice rose to yell the last part, pummelling the tunnels with its modulated tones. *Free . . . free . . . free . . .*

The last word echoed, receding slowly into silence. "Oh, dear." Reggie stopped, listening to the final reverberations. He half turned to Thibault. "My apologies. I was not constructed for stealth."

Thibault waved a hand, blinded by Reggie's bright headlamps. "Blink has more of you? How many more?"

"Oh, a number, sir, a number. I do not keep track. Counting is best left to calculators and accountants." It took two steps, then added, "And money launderers. Mustn't forget them."

"No. I suppose not."

The twin spotlights pierced the gloom of the undercity, penetrating deep into the corridor. It was quiet. Quiet, and humid, as if the tiled floors were being warmed by the flames of hell. Thibault wiped a hand across his forehead, already coated by a fine layer of sweat.

"Show me the way." Thibault raised a hand. "Silently, if you please."

"Certainly, sir!" Reggie replied in an exaggerated whisper before striding off.

The sloid's heavy footsteps made Thibault wince, each one

sounding like a gong, a beacon for any nearby skinners to follow. He listened for the telltale growls, snarls or scurrying heralding a charge of the fleshmad. If they came, Thibault wouldn't have long to flee.

Skinners had been vire once, before the Thirst consumed them, made them so desperate they fed on the black blood of their own kind. Something in that ash-flavoured liquid infected their minds and caused them to lose all reason, past their Thirst for blood and into a hunger for flesh. Lost souls. But perhaps they were the lucky ones.

Thibault pulled his reaver free from its holster. It wouldn't be much use against a pack, but one, maybe two, he could handle. Maybe.

The pair strode corridors silent with the press of time, a museum to an old world, a world before the termini. Mannequins lined darkened store windows like faceless statues, displaying wares that were now decades out of fashion.

Reggie made a turn into a narrower corridor, a few metres wide at most, and stopped. "My directive ends up ahead, sir." He raised an arm to point. "Ahead lies a Barren I cannot penetrate."

Thibault frowned. "A Barren, down here?"

"Yes, sir. Madam believes it to be of Jupiter's creation, to hide from Trinity eyes."

Thibault grunted, staring down the long passage. The Barrens were slip dead zones—areas containing a nullifier, a device capable of eliminating transmissions from the mimics saturating every surface of the bleed. Sloids had onboard cameras to compensate, but a decent nullifier disabled those signals too. It meant that from within the slip, the area ahead appeared as a grey, undefined wash. Inside, Reggie would be blind.

"So where do I go from here? How do I find Olympus?"

"Madam provided me with instructions. Shall I play them, sir?"

Thibault gave a sharp nod. "Yes, let's hear it."

"When the tiles underfoot are loose, take a left." Blink's voice rose from the sloid, flecked with static, sounding tinny. *"Twelve steps later, turn right. Count out sixty-four steps, take another right. Keep on until you hear the breath of the underworld, then follow it. Descend into the ground on an elevator, and you will have found Olympus."*

Reggie's own voice resumed. "Shall I replay it for you, sir?"

"Yes, once more."

The soundbite played again, and Thibault committed the instructions to memory. *Loose, left. Twelve, right. Sixty-four, right. Breath, left. Descend.*

Reggie attempted a flourishing bow with little success. "Godspeed, sir! I sincerely doubt we will ever see you again, so please know, had Madam ordered it, I would gladly have pulped you!"

"Good to know, kin." Thibault didn't keep the wryness from his tone.

With that, the silver sloid swung away, clanking back into the wider understreet, its footsteps receding into a pounding echo. With the departure of Reggie's headlamps, Thibault's night vision dominated, colouring the deserted storefronts with speckled greys and dull greens.

Thibault had no sense of when he entered the Barren. Under the light of the city streets, the borders of a Barren were often outlined by a shimmering mist produced by the mimics themselves. The self-replicating nanobots had learned to avoid the Barrens, often clustering at the boundaries, their tiny shells occasionally reflecting the light. Down here in the dark, though, the mimics were invisible to the naked eye.

He soon found the section of shattered tiles mentioned in Blink's recording. Spiderweb cracks around a central point evidenced some past impact. He took a left from there, counted out twelve steps, and turned right. The corridors were mazelike in this sector, deep within the understreets. At one time, the soundless arcade would have bustled with activity.

Before the next right, Thibault heard voices, faint and indistinct, but unmistakable. He peered around the corner. The muted tones were clear enough to make out.

". . . no one is here, dolt." The feminine voice became more muffled with each word, accompanied by a shuffling noise.

"I heard yelling, I'm telling you!" A younger male voice, louder than the first.

The female replied, but it was too indistinct for Thibault to comprehend.

"Shut up, Minerva." The male's voice was receding. "If you hadn't been sleeping, you would have . . ."

The sounds trailed off, cocooning Thibault in fresh silence.

Minerva? A Roman goddess. Goddess of . . . Thibault couldn't remember. But the name was no coincidence. Not down here.

He'd found the Fourth.

CHAPTER
TWELVE

Keep on until you hear the breath of the underworld.

Thibault could hear the darkness wheezing. It whistled through the understreet like the Devil himself was panting below.

He couldn't hear the voices anymore. It was as if the pressure of the earth and stone had suffocated the sound. Standing at the entrance of an old bookstore, he noticed that the paint on the once red door was now faded and flaking. Thibault tried the handle. It was unlocked.

A battered old bell hung on a string on the other side of the doorframe, ready to chime his ending. Thibault slid his hand up, opening the door wide enough to fit his forearm. The bell teetered at the edge.

His fingers grasped the string, curling around the brass, cradling it like a live grenade. He squeezed inside, gently closing the door and releasing the bell behind him.

Shelves lined the bookshop, each bearing the rotten remnants of discarded stock. The air smelled musty, like mould left to bake in the burn. It was quiet. Where had the owners of those voices gone?

Only one other door led from the store, between a set of tall shelves towards the back. Thibault strode over the warped hardwood floor, the stench of the old world consuming his nostrils. Marina would have hated this place, the decay of knowledge. She'd loved to read, loved sitting next to the window with the sun shining, curled up with a book and a hot cup of chamomile.

The office door was a darkened rectangle amidst crumbling plaster. Thibault sidled up to it, pressing his ear against the pine. Voices murmured on the other side. Not close, but somewhere nearby, muffled by the wooden barrier.

He slipped inside, and the voices resolved immediately.

". . . missing out. Orcus will gorge tonight." The male voice was high-pitched and whiny.

"Yeah, well, someone has to watch the entrance. You'd best keep your mouth shut if you want your Feast time, Faunus." Female. Older. She sounded bored, sleepy.

Good.

A jagged cave was carved into the opposite wall, bending away to the left. Thibault crept over to the entrance.

Within, someone scoffed. "You going to keep using those stupid names, even up here? Jupiter can't hear us, *Minerva.*"

The female's voice took on a hard edge. "Don't talk your traitorous trash around me. If I get Feast time for playing along with a dumb new name and a few hours watching an empty hole, I'm all in. The Fourth is a damned sight better than trading with the Trinity to get your taste. Keep your squawker shut, or I'll tell Jupiter someone tried to get through and splattered you in the process." Her voice became squeaky. "'I did everything I could, Jupiter, but Faunus met a brave ending.'" Her tone lowered again. "I'll make it a great story, kid. Don't you worry."

The cave curved around to the right, a warm orange glow invading the darkness up ahead. The voices were close now. Were there only two? Thibault palmed the reaver from its holster. Two, he could handle.

"Not everyone thinks it's such a good trade." Faunus' tone

had the ring of petulance. He, at least, wouldn't be a problem. Minerva would be tougher.

"Pffft, bunch of idiots, running off and disappearing like that. Feel free to leave too, kid. I won't stop you."

"Don't call me kid. I'm almost as old as you are."

"Two hundred years old or twelve, you still look like a kid. And you whine like one too."

A lit cavern opened up ahead. Not large, but more expansive than the corridor Thibault crept along. A shadow danced on the wall, vaguely vire in shape. Apart from the shadow, he couldn't make the pair out yet.

"Maybe something will happen to *you*, Minerva, if you keep talking down to me like that."

"Not even on your best night, kid. Sit down or piss off."

There was a long moment of silence, the shadow motionless on the wall. Then it moved, accompanied by a scraping sound.

"Good boy."

Thibault entered the cavern, reaver at the ready. Faunus looked young—real young—maybe fourteen physical? The woman would have been closer to forty when she Turned. Both wore shabby togas of a coarse flaxen cloth. Jupiter sure had committed to his fantasy.

The kid's mouth dropped open, exposing his fangs, his gaze immediately locking on to the barrel of the reaver levelled at Minerva's back.

She took longer to react, not seeing Thibault at first, noticing the look on the kid's face instead. "What's up with you?"

The kid lifted a single digit, half pointing it in Thibault's direction, like he didn't want to commit to it fully. Thibault reached the woman before she could turn, pressing the barrel into the back of her skull.

"What the—" She cut herself off. Nothing like a loaded weapon to smother a conversation.

"Way I figure it, you've got two choices." Thibault twisted

the reaver, driving it into the bone. "First choice: get up, leave your weapons, get out of here."

"Who the fuck are you?" Minerva turned her head until the barrel met her temple, her eyes bulging, trying to catch a look at Thibault.

"Second choice is a lot messier. But a lot faster for me." He stared straight at Faunus. "Choose."

The kid stood up, raising his hands, eyes round as moons. "I'm leaving. Just . . . don't end me."

Thibault wasn't paying attention to him, though. He saw Minerva tense, ready to leap.

She lunged to the side. The reaver roared. Thibault's reflexes intercepted before his mind caught up. Blood and brain matter slapped the cavern walls and floor, a fine black mist drifting in the wake of violence.

Thibault held back a curse. If more goons were hanging around nearby, they would have heard that for sure. His was not a weapon of stealth or subtlety.

"You gave us a choice!" The kid yelled from near the entrance, but he didn't do more than complain, didn't even lower his hands. Smart.

Thibault glanced at him. "She chose, kin—just not with words."

Faunus backed away to the cave entrance and bolted as soon as he had the opportunity. Messy, letting the kid go, but Thibault was no murderer. Not yet, anyway.

He waited for the footsteps to fade before holstering the reaver, then stepped over Minerva's body and crossed the room. On the far side of the wall, a wire-mesh door sat embedded in the rock face, an open-frame elevator beyond. Inside, a single lever was stuck in the up position.

Thibault slid back the gates and entered, then jammed the lever to one side. The elevator shuddered into motion, bearing him down into the bowels of Olympus.

CHAPTER
THIRTEEN

The elevator shaft was deep, the steel cage clanking the entire way down. Damned thing made so much noise, it was sure to wake the underworld. Thibault thumbed his reaver, palm resting against the titanium-alloy stock.

The further the elevator descended, the hotter he felt. Twitchy, like his muscles couldn't relax. Hard to loosen up when your ending might be waiting at the end of the ride.

The air became stale. Not the stale of the city, where it sat under the Veeshield baking in the sweat and sorry of the citizens. Stale like the earth had drawn all the life from it, squeezed it dry. Limp. Lifeless. The Fourth were down here somewhere, breathing this same air.

The walls pressed in on Thibault, the rock between him and the surface settling on his mind, heavier with each passing second. Suddenly, light carved its way into the elevator cage, sluicing up from the bottom until it revealed a bricked room. Built of limestone? Thibault blinked, momentarily blinded by the glare, and yanked his reaver clear.

The elevator juddered to a stop with a loud clang, a cloud of dust puffing into the air.

Silence. A silence so pure it pulsed in Thibault's eardrums, like they'd invented their own sound to make up for the lack, desperate for stimulation.

No one waited for him. A brick corridor arced away in front of him, lined on each side by repeating electric lights styled like flaming torches, each one swelling, fading, and flickering. The hefty stone blocks composing the walls, floor and ceiling had each been laid with precision. Someone had spent a lot of time down here carving out an odd habitat.

Thibault heaved the elevator's wire door open, the clatter splitting the air like unexpected gunfire. If his chrome palms could sweat, they would have been dripping. He wiped away the perspiration beading on his forehead.

He crept into the squat corridor. The torchlight pooled at eerie intervals, lending the stone brickwork a texture of threat. It curved around to a crossroads, two more passages leading off on either side. Neither hinted at their destination, so Thibault continued straight on, for lack of a better idea.

Around a corner, he met a heavy golden door, webbed by an intricate flaring pattern radiating out from a muscled figure at the nexus. Lightning bolts, Thibault realised. Jupiter didn't lack for ego.

He eased the door open. Voices rose from within, indistinct, increasing in volume with the widening of the portal. Thibault followed the echoing sounds, winding through another corridor, passing yet another crossroads. The underground labyrinth appeared immense, like a second undercity crawling beneath the first. If he needed to leave in a hurry, he could easily wind up getting lost trying to find his way back.

Shadows danced ahead through a cavernous opening, vaguely humanoid figures stretching up the walls, indistinct silhouettes cast in a fitful orange glow. The passage spilled into an expansive oval gallery, like a hollowed-out egg, rounded above and flat below. Many identical entrances dotted the walls of the chamber, with curving stairs surrounding the centre like in a stadium.

A middling crowd milled around on the floor of the great chamber, garbed in flaxen togas like their comrades from the world above. Thibault quickly counted. Around fifty vire, a mixture of backgrounds and physical ages. Their voices were hushed, expectant, a crowd waiting for a show to begin. But what was the show? And who would be the star?

He ran his gaze over the rest of the chamber. Actual flaming torches lit this space—unlike the electric ones he'd seen in the underground maze—the flames licking and dancing, responsible for the jittery shadows and warm light. A circular chasm plunged away into the centre of the chamber, deep enough that Thibault couldn't see the bottom from his vantage point. What was down there?

Affixed to the roof sat a circular disc, roughly the size of a sloid's visor. Around its circumference, edge work flared like sharpened ducts, the air around the device warped like a heat haze. Thibault knew its purpose on sight.

A nullifier. The device that created the Barren for Olympus, hiding them from Trinity eyes. The reason Reggie had been unable to follow.

The crowd stirred, drawing Thibault's attention. Seconds later, a towering figure marched into the cavern from the side opposite where he was standing, the heels of his boots bellowing around the chamber.

Thibault knew he'd found Jupiter. The way his deep-browed gaze roamed the space, the poise of his chiselled chin, the sneer hovering at the corners of his lips—this was a leader used to being obeyed, and one who revelled in the leading.

Jupiter strode to the front of the crowd before the black pit, raising his powerful arms overhead, two golden-gloved fists shining in the torchlight, gilded bracers wrapping his forearms. "Mighty Orcus hungers for the unworthy!"

The crowd erupted with cheers, roaring, fists pumping into the air. Jupiter let them continue for several moments, head arched like a preening cat basking in the tumult. He raised his gleaming hands again, palms out, gesturing for calm.

"A rare night for the Underworld. Two souls set to be judged by mighty Orcus. One of our own requires judgement for her betrayal and broken oaths. And the other . . ." Jupiter raised his voice. "An intruder has dared to defile the halls of Olympus!"

The crowd roared in reply. Thibault froze, muscles tensing to tightened cords. Jupiter knew he was here? How? Thibault primed himself to bolt back to the elevator, visualising the path he had to take.

"First, bring out the betrayer!"

A pair emerged from the other side of the forum, a male vire garbed in the style of a Roman legionary dragging out a smaller female. Her legs slid along the stone floor, the sound of her weeping filling the oval dome.

Jupiter's voice quieted, but it carried over the vire's crying. "Just as Tarpeia tried to betray Rome to the Sabines, our own Decima would betray us to damnation."

"No . . . no . . . Please, Lord Jupiter, no . . ." The woman keened like a wounded hound pleading with its master.

"You would have freed the Titans, Decima! Led them to Olympus! You wish to destroy us, Decima? You would shatter the Fourth!"

"No!"

"You are no pillar of Fate, Decima. Olympus shall no longer provide you succour. I cast you down, down into the Underworld, to be judged by the great punisher!"

The woman screamed, sharper than any blade, the sound tearing through Thibault's mind. "No! Please, my Lord Jupiter . . . No!"

The woman flailed against her captor and wrenched herself free, slipping from his grasp. The guard tried to grab her, but she fled his reach, sprinting for the nearest exit.

She was going to escape. Thibault willed power into her limbs, clenching his fists. He didn't care what transgression she'd committed. He doubted it would compare to the retribution Jupiter sought.

A burst of light blinded Thibault. A sharp crack split the air. A shriek battered his eardrums.

He blinked against the flash, a jagged afterimage burned into his vision. To Thibault's eyes, it led from Jupiter to the woman, connecting them with inverted luminance. Burning flesh wafted to Thibault's nostrils, a smell like charred chicken mixed with ozone.

Jupiter lowered his right arm, his hand contorting unnaturally. No, not contorting. Reassembling.

As Thibault watched, Jupiter's fist reconfigured itself. Fingers appeared, then a thumb, and in a heartbeat, the whole golden glove returned.

An augment. Was this Blink's work? Her weapon? What the Fourth had kidnapped her to do? To create lightning at Jupiter's fingertips? Like slime on a snail, it was a match for the leader's ego.

Decima squirmed on the limestone floor, one of her legs blasted clean away at the knee, a charred ruin where flesh and bone had been.

"You cannot flee judgement, Decima. You cannot flee the Fourth." Jupiter's voice cut through her wailing. "Cast her into the Underworld."

Several members of the crowd broke off to help the legionary. They snatched at the woman and hoisted her above their heads, ignoring her piteous howls. She begged forgiveness, pleaded with Jupiter to spare her, to let her prove her worth once more. But he turned his back, facing the dark pit in the centre of the chamber, a hungry exultance coating his bluff features.

Thibault had a sick feeling, a premonition of what was about to happen. The crowd surged forward, seething around the pit like an angry tide, ants desperate to please their queen. The woman's screams redoubled, but squirm as she might, her strength wasn't enough.

Thibault clamped his teeth together, feeling his jaw creak with the pressure. At some point, his hand had grasped the stock of his reaver.

There was nothing he could do. He could rush in, gun booming, send a few on the next journey, but it wouldn't help the woman. Whatever path had led her here had run its course, an unstoppable, winding river, unable to break its banks. She needed a hero, not a hound.

The woman hurtled out over the lip of the pit, limbs flailing for salvation. They found none. The chasm swallowed her cries, focusing them to harrowing echoes. A thud choked the howls off. Seconds later, a groaning sob of pain emerged from the depths, the sound of someone who knew fate had turned its unforgiving back on them.

Thibault didn't have long to wonder what would happen next. A growl replied from the pit, something emerging from the deep within a saliva-sodden throat, soaked with hunger. Thibault had heard growls like that before.

A skinner. The realisation made his stomach rebel, bending him double, as if his mind had served his guts an eviction notice. The Fourth fed their enemies to skinners, fed the madness infecting their reason.

He'd seen enough. He wouldn't find the clues to Fortuna's ending listening to Decima's grisly demise. Thibault turned his back on the chamber, on the ripping flesh and shredding tendons and the frenzied baying of the crowd.

Then he came face-to-face with Faunus, the kid he'd let go.

"Over here! My Lord Jupiter! An intruder! He ended Minerva!"

The boy's face gleamed with feral triumph. Thibault had made a major miscalculation.

CHAPTER
FOURTEEN

Thibault jerked the reaver from its holster and fired both rounds at Faunus, but the boy ducked around the corner. The shots slammed into limestone, shards exploding.

Thibault ran without looking back. His hand dove into his trench for more shells, emptying the spent pair without a glance.

Faunus leapt at him from the corner, but Thibault was ready for it. He hammered his left arm into the boy's side, the strength of the augmented limb overwhelming his attacker's limited momentum, sending Faunus hurtling backwards.

Thibault didn't pause. He sped for the corner—

The world flashed white.

Pain annihilated thought.

His heart stopped.

Thibault spun, launched into the air. His back crashed into the wall, hammering his spine. The floor broke his fall, knocking the wind from his lungs.

His left arm lost all feeling, pain radiating through his chest from the grafts at his shoulders, throbbing with dull flames. After a moment, his heart kicked in again like a bucking goat. Thibault gasped, a sudden tidal wave of blood ploughing through his veins.

Jupiter. Jupiter's lightning had struck him.

He needed to move. Thibault rolled, wedging a foot beneath him, vision smeared like warped glass bricks. He got no further.

Someone tackled him, bearing him to the stone floor. Thibault's lungs decompressed, and he struggled for air.

"Another intruder within our anointed halls!" Jupiter's voice boomed. "Orcus shall feed well!"

♦

Thibault tried to struggle against his captors, but action refused to follow thought. They dragged him through the limestone corridors and pools of flickering torchlight. A blackened spot marred his left forearm, the nanofilm melted and ruined from the lightning strike. It twitched at his mental urges, refusing to obey.

Webs of pain radiated from his shoulder grafts, scouring the rest of him. Every nerve cell felt flayed in the aftermath.

They rounded another turn. Iron bars stretched from floor to ceiling, embedded in stone, each thick as a shot glass. Four heavy gates stood on either side, one for each cell. Thibault made a last lurch to rip himself free, but his strength had fled into the darkness, lost and alone. He wasn't sure his captors had even noticed his efforts.

A legionary marched to the cell door and wrenched it open with a loud squeal. Thibault hurtled through the iron portal, thudded into the wall, and sank to his knees before his pride could protest. The gate slammed shut, a key turning in the heavy lock, and his captors swung away with a final sneer.

He'd been in worse situations. At least he thought he had. It was hard to think right then. If he could escape a terminus, he could escape a jail cell hundreds of metres underground.

Yeah. Sure. Right after he'd gotten some rest.

His eyelids drooped, and he collapsed. Sleep welcomed him home.

CHAPTER
FIFTEEN

"You'd best wake, boyo."

The tunnel rumbled with a resonant voice, prodding Thibault's consciousness. A silhouette in the distance ran towards the light, pushing further and further, desperate to reach it, hands outstretched. But Thibault knew they never would. It was too far, the tunnel too expansive. Trapped too long.

"Won't be long until they come."

The voice ushered Thibault upwards, the sonorous tone helping his thoughts break the surface. The image of the tunnel faded before the stone cell invaded.

Thibault blinked, the faux torchlight harsh against his waking pupils. He shifted, expecting his body to complain, but found it stiff rather than sore. How long had he slept, that his vire healing had responded to the damage from Jupiter's weapon?

Thibault rolled himself over, propping his back against the wall, legs lying haphazardly in front of him, knees bent. Surprisingly, he could flex his left arm. A jet-black mark marred the forearm, radiating sooty streaks, the sensory nanofilm melted like burned plastic. It left a great hole in his senses, like a hunk of his arm was missing, his brain battling to reconcile what he saw.

But miraculously, the arm had returned to function, obeying Thibault's commands. It must have rebooted while he slept. Blink knew her augments, he'd give her that.

A hulking brute watched from the next cell. Two beady eyes observed Thibault from a face that wouldn't look out of place on an axe handle, the nose flat and broad below a brow as sheer as a cliff face.

"Who are you?" Thibault's voice was dry, the sound scraping across his throat, barely audible.

It didn't seem to faze the giant vire. "Name's Tyre, not that it matters none. What's yours?"

"Who's coming?"

A wry smile curved the giant's large lips, exposing the most impressive set of fangs Thibault had ever seen. "Manners rot at the end, eh?"

"I'm Thibault. Answer the question. Who's coming?"

Tyre chuckled like a bass guitar. "Not the sharpest blade in the kitchen, are we? Don't you know where you are?"

Thibault kept a rein on his irritation. If the brute could help, Thibault needed to keep him on his side. "The Fourth. Olympus."

The grin faded from Tyre's face. "Ya, you got that aright. So, you know who's coming."

"How do you know they're coming?"

"Got a sense for time, even down here." A finger the size of the bars on their cells tapped the side of Tyre's broad head. "Said they'd come in the morning. Want to feed my brother when the sun's staggering to her feet."

Thibault tried to keep the surprise from his face but realised he'd failed when Tyre continued, his heavy brow folding over itself. "You know where we're going then, eh?"

"Your brother? Orcus?"

Tyre's blue eyes flashed, lit by cold wrath. Thibault was

suddenly glad for the iron bars keeping them separated. "His name's Max, not . . . what that shiny prick up there calls him."

"He's a skinner." Thibault said it as gently as he could, which admittedly was pretty rough, given the current circumstances.

The giant shook his massive head, strands of lank white hair rolling about his skull. "I know that. But he's still my brother. He ain't no one's toy, skinner or no."

Thibault studied Tyre's face. A barely concealed anger bubbled under the bluff exterior, but a sense of defeat also emanated from the big vire, like he'd already given up.

"You came down here to save him? Save your brother?"

Tyre squinted at him. "What of it?"

"Nothing." Thibault shrugged. "Admirable. I guess."

Heat infected Tyre's voice now. "You guess."

Sighing, Thibault closed his eyes and rested his head against the wall. "Seems we're both fools."

"Call yourself fool. Not me."

Thibault gave a slight nod, opening his eyes again. "My apologies. It shouldn't be foolish to try to save the ones you love. But the world makes it hard to see it any other way."

Tyre grunted and shifted where he sat, for the first time looking a little uncomfortable. "Big bastard always had more heart than sense. Always leaping in to help, especially if it were a woman doing the asking."

Pieces clicked together in Thibault's mind. "Blink sent Max here."

Tyre eyeballed him. "She sang her song for you too? You don't strike me as the white knight type."

"Thanks," Thibault said in a wry tone. Then he shook his head. "But you're right. I'm no hero."

"So why're you here?"

Thibault brushed dust off his pants. He used the moment to consider his answer. What harm was the truth when he was already at the bottom of a pit? "Came to end Jupiter."

Tyre's eyes widened for a moment, then he burst out

laughing. The sound hammered the walls. "You should've come with an army. Little underprepared, wouldn't you say?"

Thibault ignored the laughter. "And I came to find out what happened to someone. Someone who got ended. A woman."

The other vire grunted. "Mystery solved, then. Sorry, boyo. Bad way to go, but Max . . . he ain't himself."

"No, it wasn't your brother, wasn't Orc—Max. She was meshed when it happened."

Tyre nodded slowly, his blunt forehead creased with a frown. He opened his broad mouth to say something more, but whatever it was died in his throat when the sound of scuffing feet echoed up the corridor.

The noise resolved into a group of Jupiter's legionaries. Thibault counted quickly. Eight. He recognised several of them from the crowd in the chamber.

Tyre rose to his feet in the next cell, leg muscles bulging under his pants. At full height, he stood easily two feet taller than any of their captors, and twice as wide. Thibault had no desire to fight him, that was for damned sure. Hopefully Max was the runt of their abnormally large litter. Knowing his luck of late, though, he doubted it.

"Don't you give us any trouble, now," one of the legionaries said through the bars, watching Tyre with narrowed eyes. His voice was high-pitched and reedy, like his vocal cords were stretched thin as paper. "You won't see your brother again if you do, you hear?"

The giant's big lips spread across his face in a wide smirk, beady eyes widening with a maddened light. He brought his hands together, clenching one fist in the other, bones cracking in an unpleasant way.

"No trouble, little lad. No trouble at all." Tyre's voice was thick with threat, and the air thrummed with the giant's bass. He put on a good show, no doubt. Although, Thibault considered, it probably wasn't a show.

The group of vire at Tyre's cell door paused, each of them

shifting their weight, eyeballing the occupant. Thibault couldn't blame them. His fellow captive looked like he could end all eight of them with his bare hands.

The one in front drew a weapon—Thibault's weapon. His reaver. The legionary levelled it at the giant through the bars.

"I'm gonna open these doors, boys, and when I do, you stroll out nice and meek-like, you hear?"

The one with the reaver unlocked Tyre's cell and waved at him to leave. The giant ambled forward, apparently following orders, until he reached the armed vire. He stared down his nose at the guard. The legionary's sallow face pinched as he craned his neck to look up.

Tyre's hand whipped out, snatching the guard's wrist and sweeping it to one side. The reaver roared, a charged shot blasting out, ricocheting from the wall. Tyre held on to the guard's arm while the guard stared back, his mouth open like a stunned salmon.

"Stop right th—"

The captive legionary didn't get to finish his sentence. A balled fist thundered into his stomach like an eighteen-wheeler. Air whooshed from flattened lungs. Thibault was fairly certain he heard some ribs break.

The guard reeled, and Tyre let him go, a meaty fist snatching up the reaver. The legionary choked, clutching at his stomach, doubled over. He convulsed and vomited a jet of yellow bile onto the floor.

Tyre tossed the reaver to one of the other guards. "Best be about it then, lads." He strode off without looking back.

CHAPTER
SIXTEEN

The guards watched Tyre walk away through the torch-lit limestone corridor, confusion painted on every face. A few glanced at Thibault nervously as they unlocked his cell.

Thibault offered them an apologetic shrug for their comrade, who was kneeling on the floor, then jogged to catch up to Tyre. The giant's face was set like granite.

Leaning in, Thibault whispered, "You didn't have to give my reaver back, kin."

Tyre's eyebrow arched, but he didn't look over. "One shot against eight? We both know you wouldn't make it, boyo, cowards or no."

He had a point. Thibault didn't bother to reply, instead working on memorising where they were going, the layout of the corridors. Once they'd walked by a few familiar passages, he was fairly sure where they were in relation to the elevator, but he couldn't be certain. They were all so damned similar. He had the impression of being buried in the centre of an anthill, ushered along by soldiers to their queen, the surface leagues above.

That wasn't so far from the truth.

Their guards didn't lead them to the oval chamber like Thibault had expected. Instead, they wound through a maze of corridors with too many twists and turns for him to track. Finally, they stopped outside a pair of massive golden doors. In the centre, a motif of lightning blasted out from a towering figure, webs of jagged bolts launching over the heads of an undulating crowd.

Why was it that whatever compelled people to lead and subjugate also drove them to create works that were far more ostentatious than necessary? Was it simply ego? A fear of being forgotten, or being irrelevant? The smallest minds left the biggest landmarks.

Two of the guards pushed the heavy doors open, while another gestured with the reaver for the prisoners to enter. The one Tyre had punched hung back, clutching his nose with a sour expression. Probably didn't want to risk a repeat. Thibault didn't blame him.

Jupiter preened behind an ornate gilded desk that sported curved legs and feet shaped like a lion's paws. Thibault hated it on sight.

Jupiter's handsome face broke into a wide smile when he looked up. He rose from the desk, striding around to stand before them. His hands were clasped behind his back, his defined pectorals thrust out, proclaiming his virile masculinity. He'd cropped his white hair at the front in that old Roman style. It was so greasy it appeared grey.

The would-be god regarded Thibault with a sly smirk, apparently amused. Except, behind his eyes was a gleam that Thibault recognised—a savage glint, corrupted by madness, promising violence.

"I understand why the brute invaded my domain," Jupiter said. "A misguided attempt to save a brother who already ascended." Tyre growled deep in the back of his throat, but Jupiter ignored him, focusing on Thibault. "But you are a curiosity, hound. Do you come seeking a thrall amongst my flock?"

Thibault froze his features in place, trying not to give away his surprise. He hadn't expected Jupiter to recognise him. How much did this golden fool know of what happened on the surface, away from the safety of his underground?

Jupiter strolled closer. "Are you here for one of mine, hound? Have you come to take my children from me?" He stopped in front of Thibault and bent his neck down until their faces were level. His voice dropped, low and quiet. "Or have you come for me, hmm? Are the so-called Trinity feeling threatened?" He raised his head again, the lines around his eyes hardening, that glint sparkling bright. "Speak."

Thibault considered his options. He could play to Jupiter's arrogance, pretend this little group of sycophants had come under the ire of one of the Trinity Families. But what could he gain from that angle? Likely, Jupiter would send pieces of Thibault Allard back to a bemused enforcer. Perhaps he would even send them to Condrite.

No. Thibault had a different card to play. "I came to find out what you did to Fortuna."

It was Jupiter's turn to be surprised. There was a slight widening of his eyes before he controlled his features. It lit a signal fire for Thibault.

"Fortuna?" Jupiter rolled her name on his tongue like that of an old lover. "And who has hired you to find my wayward daughter? Does jilted Condrite seek his lost flame?"

Time to play dumb. Thibault frowned. "Condrite?"

Jupiter raised a sculpted eyebrow at Thibault, the curve to his mouth trumpeting genuine amusement. "I heard you were meticulous. No rock you wouldn't slime your way under to claim your prize." He paused, waiting for a reaction, but Thibault refused to budge. Jupiter's smile widened anyway. "Condrite is her husband, Trinity pup. If you know Fortuna, you should know that much. Or did you bed her before you knew who she was?"

Thibault allowed his eyebrows to inch upward, feigning

surprise. A stroked ego bore many fruits. "Tell me what you did with her. No games."

"I?" Jupiter puffed out his chest and pointed at himself with a languid finger. "I gave the poor soul succour from her abuser. I offered sanctuary and safety!"

"You kidnapped her, along with Blink. Don't play me for a fool."

Jupiter's laugh boomed out, his broad mouth displaying perfect white teeth and two sparkling fangs. "But a fool you are, hunter! You, who dance to the Trinity's tune when they pluck at your strings. How could you be anything more?"

"So, what did you do with her? You end her once you tired of her company? Or did one of your flock do it without your knowledge?"

The grin faded, Jupiter's eyebrows drawing down. "Tut-tut, hound. Do not insult the worthy. There are worse fates than the jaws of Orcus."

"You're lying," said Thibault. "Is there something you don't want your followers to know, God of Lies?"

For a split second, Jupiter's pupils flicked to the group of legionaries standing behind Thibault, so fast Thibault barely caught it. He'd plucked a nerve. Jupiter was hiding something, and he needed to learn what, and quickly. It could be the key to unlocking his escape.

"Enough of these games." Tyre's voice rumbled into the conversation. He slapped one fist in the other, cracking his fat knuckles. "Take me to my brother, or your pretty room will get real messy."

Jupiter's mouth tightened at the threat, and though he maintained his sickly smile, it no longer contained the mirth it had a moment before. "You have a short memory. Do you need to be reminded of whom you address?"

He raised a gleaming golden hand, flaring his fingers outward, palm up. From this close, it was clear both forearms were augmented, grafted below the elbow. The fingers retracted, disappearing into Jupiter's hand one segment at a time, the rest of the hand following, sinking away into his wrist until the entire thing vanished, replaced by a gaping hole.

Electricity crackled around the opening.

"No wonder you're so tense," Tyre said. "Must be stressful to piss with one of those things gripping your todger." He nodded at the legionaries behind them. "Or does one of them hold it for you instead?"

Jupiter's voice dropped, quiet as a forgotten tomb. "Your jokes will not spare you from judgement, child. The jaws of Orcus shall rend your flesh until you beg for salvation."

Tyre stepped forwards. A legionary grabbed his shoulder, but the giant ignored it. "Take me to him. Play your games if you must, but have your slaves take me to the pit."

"Slaves? My court are not slaves, child. No. The true slaves" —Jupiter thrust a finger towards the ceiling—"are up there. Slaves to their nature, unable to rise above. But we . . ." He spread his arms wide, slowly spinning in a circle, face raised. "We in Olympus have ascended beyond simple flesh. The true slaves dwell above in Tartarus, willingly led, on leashes they fastened to themselves."

"Is that why you let your people use the mesh?" Thibault cut in. "Because they're free?"

The exultation on Jupiter's face faded, and he lowered his hands back by his sides, turning to regard Thibault. "It takes time to ascend from"—his pupils flicked up and down, accompanied by a sneer—"our baser selves. Some are too weak even then, like your Fortuna."

Thibault crossed his arms. He had to take the bait. "What do you mean? What happened to her?"

Jupiter allowed himself a clenched grin. "She fled back to Tartarus, Trinity dog. Fled from sight, fled from mind. She is a slave once more, denied the gifts of Olympus. Another meaningless fool in your master's menagerie."

"She's no thrall. Someone ended her."

Jupiter's lip twitched. "And you are her avenging saviour, hound? On a quest for righteous vengeance?"

"There's nothing righteous about what I do. I'm not delusional. Not like some."

Tyre chuckled, throaty and malicious.

Jupiter's eyes flashed, but his face broke into a smile that made all his previous expressions seem childlike by comparison. "There's only one thing that separates delusion from reality, hunter." His fangs glittered in the electric torchlight. "Belief." He leaned forwards. "Believe hard enough, long enough, invest all of yourself into it, and you can make anything real. As real as you or I, or the oversized ape here."

Jupiter turned away from them, casting his gaze around the room. "I have made Olympus real. I have raised up the worthy, shared with them my dreams." He glanced at Tyre. "And I have made the Underworld real, with Orcus standing vigil over the souls I send below. I will make the Underworld real for you, too. And rest assured, the pain of your ending will be as real as anything you've ever experienced."

Thibault felt a chill slide along his skin, but not at the thought of his ending, or the promise of pain. If this was the end for him, it was the end for Marina too. He couldn't allow that. He couldn't allow her to pay for his mistakes. Not again.

"About bloody time, boyo." Tyre yawned. "I'm getting sleepy listening to your prattling."

"Two souls depart with the rising sun! Two wicked souls find their place in the land of the dead, where mighty Orcus shall flay them for eternity!"

Thibault noticed Tyre shifting next to him. The giant leaned down to whisper, though he kept it loud enough for the entire chamber to hear. "Talks a lot of shit for a god, doesn't he?"

They'd been ushered through to the chamber from Jupiter's rooms after their conversation, where they waited for the congregation to file in before the man himself strode in and began his theatrical speech. Thibault wondered if the preening fool had been waiting in the corridor for the right moment to appear.

"You'd think he could just"—Tyre waggled his sausage fingers in the air—"magic us into submission."

Jupiter didn't pause at the interruption. Thibault could believe Ors' claim about him being a billionaire before the Bloodscourge. The morbid fascination with melodrama matched his towering ego.

"Judgement by Orcus can be the only punishment for invading Olympus. But today, we have a special circumstance." Jupiter grinned down at them. Something in the expression made Thibault's heart grow cold, like a chill wind had wafted through the chamber.

"Today, we pit mighty Orcus against these two intruders of Tartarus for the right to don the mantle of Mars, our Lord of War." The vire's eyes shone with a feral light. "Only one shall stand, come the end. Only one shall ascend. Only one . . . shall attain the title of Mars!"

The chamber erupted in cheering, the crowd of Jupiter's followers whooping and screaming for blood. Thibault glanced at Tyre and caught the giant looking back at him with a raised eyebrow. He was suddenly glad he'd been friendly with the big vire in their cell.

Tyre leaned in. "Only way we get out of this is by working together. Don't go stabbing me in the back, eh, boyo?"

"Agreed." Thibault gave a surreptitious nod, watching Jupiter the whole time. If the pretend god guessed the pair had an alliance, he might change his plans.

Of course, Tyre could be lying. Claiming they were working together, waiting for the right moment to feed Thibault to Max. And the giant must be wondering the same thing about him.

Thibault sighed, feeling the full weight of the rock between him and the streets way above. Why could nothing be easy?

A shove in the centre of his back pitched him towards the dark pit. He noticed some of the Fourth members try the same with Tyre, earning themselves an amused look. They flinched away when Tyre raised his hand at them.

"I'm coming, brother." The giant strode forwards until they both stood at the lip of the pit.

For the first time, Thibault saw into its murky depths. It dropped away roughly five metres below them. The walls were sheer, the same stone as the rest of the complex, with nothing to grab for climbing. The only exit was a steel-barred gate cloaked too deeply in shadow to see where it led. Black stains marred every surface, like someone had been doing cartwheels with a paintbrush. Dried vire blood, and lots of it. How many had Jupiter fed to his pet?

"Ah, brother." Tyre heaved a great sigh beside him, staring down at Max's handiwork. "What have they done to you?"

Thibault opened his mouth to ask if Tyre was sure now about getting his brother out, but before he had the chance, someone shoved him in the back again.

The floor of the pit hurtled up to meet him. He slammed into the stone, knees buckling like a rag doll. He sprawled onto the ground, wind exploding from his lungs, barely catching himself from cracking his head.

A thunderous crash sounded beside him, the flagstones vibrating. Thibault glanced over, stars still dancing at the corners of his vision, noting the spiderweb of cracks in the blood-soaked stone beneath the hulking giant. Tyre had joined him.

"Bit rude." Tyre rose to his feet from his crouch, wincing with the effort.

Thibault didn't respond. It was all he could do not to pass out from lack of oxygen. But he forced himself to stand anyway, head spinning like a flushed toilet. Max could be on them at any moment. He needed to be ready.

"Return their worldly possessions!" Jupiter's mad roar reverberated around the pit, echoing off the walls. "Let their ending be both fair and glorious!"

A cloth-wrapped bundle landed on the stone next to Thibault, the items inside clinking against each other. He reached for it, a faint sliver of hope cresting the horizon of his despair. His reaver lay inside, holstered, four slake vials nestled beside it. One had shattered with the impact, leaking the milky drug into the fabric.

He snatched up the reaver first, shrugging off his trench to sling the leather holster around his torso, then drew the weapon and checked the ammo. One shell, and no more to spare. He shrugged. Better than a kick in the guts.

Thibault put his trench back on, grabbed the vials, and thrust them into the inner pocket. Maybe they'd come in handy. Hell, he could always get high if the end was near, rob the crowd of his suffering. But he wasn't there yet. Not nearly.

"What'd you get, boyo?" Tyre was standing just in front of him, between Thibault and the barred gate, slapping a blackjack against his palm. Perhaps the small weapon would be useful in a scrap, but against a skinner? Might as well piss into a firestorm.

"The other reaver shell, and three slake vials," Thibault replied.

"Slake, eh?" Tyre's eyes lit up. "Might be I have a—"

A roar cinched off his words like a concussive blast, sweeping away all conscious thought. Lurking beyond a barred gateway, a monstrous silhouette hunched out of the light. The shred of hope Thibault had felt moments ago shrivelled up and suffocated. What he could see of the dark figure was massive, at least two feet taller than Tyre—and more muscled, if that was possible.

The bars retracted into the stone ceiling of the corridor with a grating shriek. The silhouette lumbered forwards into the light.

"Hey there, brother." Grief infected Tyre's quiet tone. "You look like shit."

Predatory eyes boiled in a face of nightmare, a well of hunger within deep enough to swallow the entire world. Fangs the size of steak knives protruded from a mangled mouth, the other teeth long gone. Flesh hung in ragged strips from the monster's frame, a mess of unhealed cuts and welts, many infected and oozing pus. Skinners couldn't heal like normal vire. Their bodies wasted in concert with the flesh they consumed.

Tyre tossed aside his blackjack, apparently agreeing with Thibault's assessment of its worth, and shot a warning glance over his shoulder. "Don't hurt him. I'm getting my brother out of here. Alive."

Right. Like either was a possibility.

CHAPTER
EIGHTEEN

Max bellowed again, strings of saliva vibrating in his mouth. A few strands collected into globs, shooting through the air and arcing onto the ground, splattering the stone in the pit.

Thibault felt his bones shudder. He'd been in tighter corners before, and with longer odds. Hadn't he?

Max—though Orcus seemed more fitting somehow—lurched into a charge, heaving his enormous frame towards Tyre. Cheers rose somewhere far over their heads, the Fourth whooping for the monster to make their endings as brutal as possible. Thibault could hear Jupiter's maddened voice above the clamour, intoning more of his dramatic nonsense.

Tyre leaped to the side at the last moment, but he'd miscalculated the reach of his brother's arms. Max clutched Tyre's shirt, unable to slow his momentum, dragging the giant along behind. They crashed into the wall, a tangle of brawn and oversized limbs. Tyre clambered onto his brother's back, looping his right arm around the skinner's thick neck.

"Stick him with the slake!"

Thibault immediately recognised Tyre's daring plan. Jump on his brother's back, hold him down, and let Thibault drug him into dreamland. It might have worked too, except, at that moment, the beast decided to charge at Thibault.

The freakish skinner bore down on him, each thundering step sending a shockwave through the floor. Thibault lined up the single shot left in the reaver, aiming for Max's forehead. But he couldn't shoot. Couldn't squeeze that trigger.

If he ended Max, he'd have Tyre to deal with next. A brother out for retribution, and Thibault with no shells to spare. Never mind that he liked the muscled prisoner. Plus, even if he tried to put Tyre down, Thibault wasn't sure he could.

So he yanked a slake injector from his coat instead and flicked off the cap with his thumb. He darted aside and swung the needle into Max's bulging arm, a mess of flesh crashing past. The syringe bit deep, tearing free from Thibault's hand. But the injector compressed, sluicing salvation into the fiend.

Max and Tyre crashed into the side of the pit, their inertia too great to manoeuvre. Tyre hit the wall, tumbling from his brother's back. He scrambled to his feet and rounded on Thibault.

"Might've misjudged that," he said between breaths, giving Thibault a sheepish look. "He's a mite stronger than I recall."

Thibault didn't reply. He was watching Max turn around. A normal vire would've been out by now from a full dose, but Max appeared unfazed, like the potent drug had been simple saline.

Tyre cursed. "How many of those you got?"

"Two more."

Max bellowed, his mouth a cavern guarded by thick strands of mucus and saliva. He swiped the slake needle from his muscle with a brutish fist.

Tyre stuck out his hand. "Let me have one. We'll stick him together."

Thibault thrust an injector into the giant's hand. "We may need to put him down, kin. You know that, right?" He tapped his holster to clarify his meaning.

Tyre's irises turned to flint. "Don't tell me what I know. I'm getting my brother out of this shit heap."

Thibault didn't have time to respond. The ground shook with Max's advance. He came on slower this time, arms stretched far to either side, fingers clawed. He growled, low and guttural.

"I'll distract him, you stick him." Tyre sidestepped away from Thibault. "Hey, brother! Remember when we used to wrestle over the last slice of pie? Huh, you remember that? You'd eat it even when you were stuffed full, just so I wouldn't get some. You were a real prick, brother."

Max's sunken eyes and corded neck darted towards Tyre, tracking his brother's movement.

"That's it. You remember me, don't you? You're still in there somewhere, aren't you, Maxy?"

Max blinked twice at the name, then shook his head like he was trying to clear the noise from his eardrums. Slowly, that neck turned back to Thibault, rheumy eyes locking on, ignoring the bait.

Shit.

Thibault sank into a half-crouch, stalking the opposite way from Tyre. If he was the bait instead, so be it. Max roared again, like he knew what they were doing. Then he charged.

He moved slower than before, like he'd learned the limits of his own momentum. Thibault palmed the slake injector, glass clinking between his chrome fingers. Max bore down on him. Thibault dived—

And stopped fast, clothes caught, wrenched backward, choking him. He smacked into something solid. Max.

Thibault caught a glint of curved fangs over his left shoulder and twisted. The beast bellowed in his face, a glob of saliva whacking Thibault's right eye, stinging like battery acid.

Thibault raised the injector, squeezed his eye shut, and stabbed down. He hit something hard, but it wasn't Max's chest. The brute's other fist had caught his hand, and now it squeezed.

Glass shattered. Metal warped. The clear liquid of their

deliverance leaked through the crushing grip, dripping onto the flagstones. But Max didn't stop there. He crushed Thibault's hand further, like he was trying to punish him for the attempt.

Blink's work met the Devil's own. Chrome alloy versus skinner muscle. The strength of Blink's augment halted the brute's brawn, but the nanofilm shrieked with pain, stabbing like fine needles.

Thibault roared in concert with Max, bestial howls joining with the din of the crowd above, a cacophony of noise and pain and fury.

Something flashed over Max's shoulder, barely glimpsed. Light on metal. Max twisted, grip loosening, flinging Thibault away from him, booming with violent rage. Thibault hit the floor hard, unable to arrest his momentum, sliding on the stone.

A spent injector rose above Max's left shoulder, buried to the hilt in the muscle. Tyre had used the opportunity well.

Max spun away from Thibault, grappling at his brother. Tyre caught Max by his shoulders, one hand on either side, as the skinner did the same to him. Muscles bulged with fat black veins fit to bursting.

The brothers struggled against each other.

Tyre was losing.

His face contorted in a hot rictus of rage, flushed dark with black blood. Max's jaws snapped inches from the younger brother's wide nose. Tyre's feet lost ground, one step at a time, towards the wall.

Max was slowing, Thibault could see that. The brute was roaring less, his eyelids drooping. The slake was having an effect, but it wasn't enough. Tyre couldn't last. Even with the edge offered by the drug, Max was overpowering him.

Thibault regained his feet in time to see them reach the wall of the pit. Tyre braced his legs against it to prevent Max from reaching him with his fangs. The purchase gave Tyre the advantage he needed to hold his own, but no more than that.

The brothers stood locked together, each straining to overcome the other, neither coming out on top.

Thibault crossed the pit in a few strides, flinging back his trench and smoothly drawing the holstered reaver. He lined it up next to Max's head, side on to the hulking monster.

"No!" Tyre growled through gritted teeth. "No!"

The trigger beckoned Thibault, an end to their battle. He couldn't wait for Max to overpower his brother. If nothing else, Thibault would need Tyre to get out of Olympus. He wasn't sure he could do it on his own.

"Damn you . . . I said . . . no!"

"You can't save him. Some things, you never come back from."

Thibault creaked the trigger a bare fraction, determined to cave in Max's head. But something stopped him. Some part of him wanted Tyre to save Max. Some illogical, childish part. So he paused. Stupidly, he paused.

"Save him, kin. Save him, if you can. Otherwise . . ."

Tyre's strained gaze flicked back to his older brother, a need in them growing more urgent. "Maxy!" His voice came out a drained whisper, desperate, pleading. "I know you're in there, brother. I know it. Tell me what to do! Tell me, please!"

Max blinked again, his snarl easing to a low growl. His eyelids moved slower, slipping over bloodshot eyes. Was it because of Tyre's words, or had the slake finally taken hold? Whatever it was, the skinner inched back, forced by Tyre's strength. First one step, then another, the tide of struggle turning in favour of the smaller brother.

Max stumbled, and in a sudden rush, lurched backwards. Tyre bore down on top of him. The huge skinner closed his eyes and went limp, head falling to one side.

"Thank you, brother." Tyre sagged over the massive creature, heaving gulps of air. "Thank you."

Thibault glanced up at the silent crowd lining the pit.

"Your trial has only just begun, gentlemen." Jupiter's voice shattered the silence. "You may have set Orcus to slumber, but the terms of this competition were made plain."

A worm burrowed through Thibault's intestines, twisting his stomach in a knot. He knew what was coming next.

"Only one may rise."

Tyre looked up at Thibault.

Thibault looked down at Tyre.

And raised the reaver.

CHAPTER
NINETEEN

Thibault aimed the gun at Max's lolling head, lined up between the titanium sights. Time to gamble.

"Hey now, boyo." Tyre frowned up at the reaver, lifting one hand, palm out.

Thibault raised his voice, enough to echo out of the pit and into the cavernous chamber above. "Let us go, Jupiter, or lose your pet skinner."

Tyre's features hardened, his muscles going still. Thibault shot him a warning look that he hoped Tyre understood. By the look on the big vire's face, he didn't.

Jupiter's laughter cut through the tension, the mocking sound bouncing off the walls, beating them down. "Which of my conditions did you not understand, hound?"

"I understood." Thibault only spoke after Jupiter's laughter had trailed off, injecting his voice with what he hoped was quiet confidence. "I also understand you didn't expect Orcus to lose."

"I admit, this turn is most surprising. If you are to become my Mars, you must understand the nature of battle. In battle's forge, fortunes turn in the blink of an eye. Or at the whim of a god. If today is the day Orcus departs the Underworld, so be it.

We shall find another! Perhaps it shall be one of you, if you prove yourself worthy of the mantle."

Thibault caught Tyre's eye, the big vire watching him with an unreadable look on his face.

Max stirred. A subtle shift, then a moan deep within the giant's chest, Jupiter's laughter rising in concert, drowning it out to anyone above. The monster was waking.

If Thibault shot Max, then Tyre would end Thibault.

If Thibault shot Tyre, Max would tear Thibault apart.

One shell. No options. The cards were played.

He'd lost.

Thibault let the reaver drop back by his side. He closed his eyes, summoning the image of Marina. Her face floated in front of him, tantalisingly close yet impossibly far. The little imperfections that made her . . . her. But were they hers, or inventions of his, grafted on by time? He would never repair those memories with reality now.

He should never have come, never met with Fortuna. Thibault let out a breath, accepting the ending that was so close, lungs deflating with his dreams. The reaver tore free from his grasp. Thibault's eyes shot open.

"Goodbye, brother." Tyre levelled the barrel at Max's head, tears streaming down the younger brother's broad face, incongruous against the harsh set of his eyes. "I know you're gone already, boyo, but I'll make it stop, all right?" His voice dropped to a whisper. "If there's a next life, I'll see you there."

The reaver boomed, a supercharged shot exiting the barrel, splintering into hundreds of fragments, caving in Max's skull and blasting out the other side. Black blood and brain smacked the stone. The huge skinner stopped moving.

Tyre tossed the spent reaver to Thibault. He caught it by the stock and slid it home into its holster beneath his trench. Not that it mattered. They were done anyway.

"Bravo!" The sound of someone clapping echoed in the pit. "Bravo! A show like no other, truly unexpected! And now for the climax—the ultimate test of mettle to see which of you can earn your place among the Fourth. I think none shall assume the mantle of Mars today, for we cannot leave the Underworld unguarded." Jupiter's voice rose, mocking and cruel. "Fight! Claim the throne! Will it be the brother or the hound?"

Thibault readied himself, preparing for Tyre's inevitable charge. He didn't think he could take the muscled vire, but he wouldn't give up without a fight. His augments against Tyre's bulk—it wasn't nothing.

"We won't be fighting today." Tyre stood, staring up at Jupiter, white-knuckled fists held by his sides. Defiant. Like a true hero. "We won't play your game, false god."

Tyre's attention was all on the crowd above. Thibault could capitalise on the distraction, take the fighter unawares. He'd have to crush the giant's skull beneath his fists, smash it to shards to end him. The only way, short of a decent weapon.

The thought stuck fast in his mind, and something slithered inside his gut in response, a sick twist of revulsion. He liked Tyre. But Tyre stood between him and Marina. He was the only way out.

Thibault took a step towards him, fingers curling into a bunched fist.

The big vire spoke again. "Are you too cowardly to come down and fight us yourself, father of the gods? Are you too impotent to do the hard work yourself?" Tyre spread his arms wide, fat fingers flared. "Come, pretender, join us in your pit. Or are you afraid? Are you cowering like a scared child?"

He raised his voice, yelling at the crowd. "King of the gods, my sweating crack! King of nothing, more like! King of an anthill!" He chuckled with dark humour. "King of cowards. King of fools."

The crowd screamed in response, howling for Tyre's ending like a pack of hungry hogs. Tyre hurled his amusement back at them.

Amazingly, it worked, the ex-billionaire's ego wounded by

the words. Jupiter landed on the flagstones, dropping into a crouch. He rose, face splitting with a predatory smirk—the smile of a grinning madman before he set to work carving up his next victim.

Tyre charged without hesitation. Thunderous footsteps pounded inside the pit.

Thibault unclenched his fist, breathing fast and shallow.

Jupiter raised his right hand. The fingers retreated into a blackened hole at the end of his golden bracer, sparks rippling around a silver ball inside.

Nothing happened. Not straight away. Tyre barrelled towards Jupiter, stretching out. Then there was a sharp crack, like the simultaneous shattering of a thousand china plates. Tyre flew backwards, rocketing into the side of the pit with the crunch of broken bones, his chest a cavernous, smoking wreckage. The big vire slumped to the side, gaze long, unseeing.

Thibault stared. Mere seconds had passed. Seconds for Tyre to scream his defiance. Seconds for Jupiter to descend and silence him.

The crowd crowed with raucous glee, a pack of hyenas screeching over a plump carcass. Their joy turned Thibault's stomach. He wanted to tear this place down, destroy this so-called Olympus bone by bone.

Jupiter turned to him, the lightning augment still exposed at the end of his forearm, sparks flitting a warning around the end. Thibault felt the whisper of his ending in that mad gaze. Tyre had been a child against this creature—less than one. What could Thibault possibly do?

"Do you also want to taunt the gods, hunter?" Jupiter strode towards him, slow, deliberate, every step heightening Thibault's tension. "Shall you goad the guardians of Olympus into granting your destruction?" Jupiter's gauntlet crackled with threat.

Thibault shook his head, watching the vire's eyes, ready to dive the instant that arm rose. It wouldn't be enough. But he'd try, anyway.

"No." Thibault eyed the augment. "There are no gods here to taunt."

"No gods?" Jupiter's voice was barely a whisper, almost inaudible.

"You're nothing new. The world has seen your like before. The only impressive thing about you is the scope of your ego and the magnitude of your delusions. Nothing more."

Jupiter's lips drew back over his fangs and teeth, the shape of a smile, the cast of a great cat. "I'd hoped for you to join us, hunter. But with an attitude like that . . . perhaps you need to truly understand the torment waiting for you in the Underworld? Orcus learned, in the end. He defied me, like you and your . . . friend. He discovered that I have more power than he could have imagined. The power of life and end. The more you struggle against my strings, the more you tangle yourself in my net."

Jupiter grinned, malice glittering on his white fangs. "Shall I feed you, hunter? Feed you charred chunks of your oversized ally until your mind is scoured by the hunger for Turned flesh?"

Thibault's mouth dried out like a vire in sunlight, ash and dust, devoid of all moisture. Fear was an old companion, so constant that Thibault often forgot it was there. He feared for Marina, feared he would never find her, never see her again.

But the fear that struck him now was animalistic, urging him to flee, setting his heart racing like a startled deer. He feared his ending because of what it meant for Marina, of course. But to become a skinner, to lose himself to something worse than the Thirst . . . That was horror beyond imagining.

Jupiter could see it, too. Like a wolf perceiving panic in its prey, he arced his lips into a joyless smirk, bathing in Thibault's terror.

Flight wasn't an option. There was nowhere to run.

Hemmed in by walls and a metal grate, never mind the maniac facing him, Thibault's nights were numbered.

So he leaped, chrome hands seeking Jupiter's throat, ready to throttle the cult leader into submission.

Jupiter backhanded him. Thibault fell, landing hard on his side.

"I know what you're thinking, hound. I won't end you. I won't make this easy. You've invaded my home and insulted my hospitality. No, easy is not written in your destiny."

Thibault surged to his feet, ready to fling himself at Jupiter again and again until the bastard was forced to put him down. Then golden fingers gripped his throat, stopping him fast.

Jupiter's hand, five-fingered once more, held Thibault in stasis, lifting him slowly from the floor until his feet dangled in mid-air.

"Feel the air choke from you, hunter. Feel the light fade from view. When you wake, you will be my new Orcus. Lesser than the last, to be sure, but that will make for more exciting judgment when I send the damned to your threshold."

Thibault tried to speak, to curse in Jupiter's face, but all he could manage was a throaty gurgle, hands scrabbling at the vire's neck. His legs kicked out, catching Jupiter in the stomach, chest, arms, but nothing loosened the pressure at his throat.

Stars danced, thousands of flecks of mixed colour smearing across his vision, a lightness at the back of his mind telling him it was okay to let go. Let go.

He used all the strength he could summon in his augmented arms to hurl a punch into Jupiter's blurry face. Then another. And another. Left and right, left and right.

Jupiter stumbled. Thibault fell.

He landed on his knees, jolts of pain shooting into his joints. Air rushed back into his lungs—wondrous, precious air—and Thibault sucked it in, inhaling despite the burning pain in his throat. He blinked, trying to clear the stars and lights, knowing that Jupiter would be upon him again soon.

The would-be god's face was a mess of blood and red welts,

one hand held up to it protectively. Thibault smiled at his work. Jupiter caught sight of the grin.

Too far. Too far to react.

"I will find another Orcus." Jupiter's voice was as mangled as his lips, but the tone that bubbled through them had lost its grandiose quality, stating a simple fact.

Jupiter's fingers retracted, folded back on themselves, cascading away. If Thibault hadn't been moments from his ending, Blink's mastery would've inspired awe. Instead, his gaze caught the silver conductor revealed inside, a spike of electrical power that was about to blast away any hope Marina had for freedom. There was nothing more he could do.

Sparks gathered around the sphere, sizzling and crackling. Thibault could only stare into it, each sparkle burning into his retinas.

It was what he deserved.

But not Marina. She deserved better.

Thibault shot up from his crouch, rushing at Jupiter, knowing he wouldn't make it but trying all the same.

From out of nowhere, Tyre looped his muscled arm around Jupiter's neck, wrenching the golden gauntlet upwards.

A sharp crack knifed the air. Blinding light exploded from Jupiter's gauntlet. Thibault slid to a stop. Chunks of charred metal rained down around him.

Tyre's body still smoked, a gaping, cauterised wound in his chest, half his face blackened and burned like an overdone steak. "Get . . . out . . ." The giant forced out the words between breaths, straining with effort. "Run!"

Another lightning blast shattered the wall, and Thibault smelled ozone. There was a scream from the crowd above.

He didn't understand. Where could he run?

Then he saw it, the yawning hole in the stone next to the barred entrance where Max had entered the pit. One of Jupiter's shots had blasted open an exit, big enough to squeeze through.

Thibault spun back towards the struggle between Tyre and Jupiter. Tyre's strength couldn't last, not in the state he was in.

"Go. Now! Leave me!"

Thibault locked eyes with the hulking giant, the strain behind them urging Thibault to go.

The hole in the wall beckoned. Through it, he saw his dark path, the path he'd trod since he'd fled the terminus. Since he'd left Marina behind. He couldn't do it again. He couldn't stay on that road. He couldn't leave Tyre too.

Thibault bolted towards the grappling pair, ducking to avoid a sweeping arc of the second golden gauntlet, both now gripped in Tyre's fists. A bolt crashed into the floor, raining flagstone fragments over Thibault, cutting his cheek.

Chrome met gold. Thibault shoved up with all the strength he could summon. Jupiter was no match for the two of them combined. Lightning streaked up, smashing into the ceiling. The crowd bellowed its raucous rage down into the pit.

Jupiter's features contorted, a dark vein throbbing in his thick neck. Thibault braced himself, helping Tyre direct Jupiter's right fist towards the pretend god's own face. Let the prick feel it for himself.

Jupiter's knee rammed into Thibault's groin. Agony exploded from his crotch. His grip faltered.

The golden bastard shoved Thibault away enough to plant his foot in Thibault's stomach and heave. The sudden decompression made Thibault projectile vomit, and he flew backwards. He hit the stone floor and skidded, metal arm dragging on stone, throwing up sparks.

Thibault levered himself up in time to see Jupiter headbutt Tyre over and over and over, black blood spraying with each crunch. Tyre finally weakened enough for Jupiter to spin and throw off his assailant. The giant stumbled, hand hovering before his ruined face. With his chest blasted half away, he looked like an animated corpse.

Thibault rose to his feet. If this was his time, he'd be damned if he greeted it on his knees.

Jupiter chuckled. Golden bracers rose, one each for Thibault and Tyre, both ports crackling, increasing in intensity. When would those damned batteries run out of juice?

Tyre hawked and spat, lobbing mucus, and spit at Jupiter's feet. "Face me without those toys and we'll see who's the better."

Jupiter grinned, white teeth smeared with his own jet blood. "Why would I do that? No . . . I think the only one to rise shall be me."

Lightning forked from the gauntlets.

CHAPTER
TWENTY

Despite himself, Thibault closed his eyes before the impact, the battle pit of Olympus and his executioner disappearing from sight. Tyre wouldn't survive another strike, and Thibault wouldn't be far behind.

But the bolt never connected. At least not with Thibault. Bright white flashed behind his eyelids, and it took him a moment to register that he remained whole. His eyes shot open.

Reggie stood before the pair of them, arms outstretched. Electricity coruscated over the silver sloid's chassis, vanishing after a moment. "I say, sir, that is no way to treat guests!"

Jupiter frowned at Reggie, the shocked expression on his face matching Thibault's own roiling emotions.

Reggie took a step forwards. "Please desist, sir. The Madam wishes for me to detain you."

Tyre grunted. "I guess reinforcements have arrived." He pointed at Jupiter. "Time to come down off your mountain."

Jupiter snarled and raised both sparking gauntlets at the sloid, unleashing a barrage of bolts. Each struck Reggie in a different location, all to no effect.

Reggie's silver chassis swallowed the electrical charges, siphoning them out of existence. "Manners, sir! I say!"

Realisation clicked for Thibault. Blink had made both Reggie and the gauntlets. Somehow, she'd made Reggie invulnerable to them.

Jupiter's hands thrust back into view, reconstructing themselves at the ends of his bracers, bunched into fists. "Come, metal fool. You think one sloid is a match for a god?"

Reggie half bowed. "My deepest apologies, sir." He raised a hand up, and only then did Thibault notice that the crowd above had quieted. "But I did not come alone."

Thibault gazed up to where a row of figures lined the sides of the pit, assorted parts cobbled together to form complete sloids. A ragtag army of junkyard electronics, each sporting various Trinity colours mixed with an assortment of silvers, browns and even faded green.

Above their heads, Thibault saw the reason for the sloid's sudden appearance. The nullifier stuck to the ceiling was a smoking wreck of twisted metal and wiring, a gaping hole blasted into the underside. One of Jupiter's own lightning bolts must have destroyed it during their struggle, allowing Blink's sloids to navigate their way down.

"We must insist, sir." The sloids spoke in tandem, each using Reggie's supercilious tone, a rolling warble that reverberated around the pit. "Come quietly, or a pulping may be necessary."

Thibault almost laughed out loud. Almost.

Jupiter stared up, mouth agape, fists still raised. Three of the Reggie clones jumped down, slamming into the flagstones lining the pit.

Jupiter flinched with each crashing addition. He paused for a moment, looking from one sloid to the next. Then he ran. The false god bolted for the hole in the wall, leaping through and off into the darkness from which Max had emerged. The three sloid clones sprinted after him, leaving the original in the pit with Thibault and Tyre. Reggie turned to face them. "Apologies for our tardiness, sirs."

"No apology necessary." Tyre spoke in a tight voice,

clutching his ruined chest, sweat streaming down his face. "I think I might have a lie down now."

His eyes rolled back in his head, and he collapsed in a heap.

CHAPTER
TWENTY-ONE

By the time Thibault and Reggie had dragged Tyre through the darkened corridors and up to the main chamber, Jupiter's followers had all fled from Blink's makeshift army. Whether deeper into Olympus or up to the surface, crammed in the elevator, Thibault was too exhausted to care.

Jupiter himself had been captured by the ragtag sloids, bruised and bloodied, his gauntlets shattered. The once-god sat on his knees with his arms held fast by a brown-and-blue sloid.

Thibault eased Tyre onto the stone floor, glad to be free of the huge vire's weight. Tyre's chest wound was hideous, three ribs shattered beyond recognition, his left lung visible and heaving beneath a layer of black ichor. It would heal eventually, given time, but Blink's surgical aid would speed his recovery.

"You were lucky, boy. Very lucky." One sloid stood gazing down into the pit. It was a motley thing, with cobalt-coloured Ortrea legs, a silver chest plate, and a crimson Anuthuma helmet.

This sloid's voice didn't sound like the others, though. It was warped by the static buzz of a modulation algorithm, but without the haughty tenor.

Thibault frowned. "Blink?"

The sloid turned to regard him, then angled its visor to Tyre's unconscious face. "He looks like Max. They're brothers?"

"Were."

Blink sighed, static warping at the sound. "I tried to pay him to come here, to save Fortuna for me, to ease my guilt. But he wouldn't take the chits. Damned fool. Damned heroic fool. And look what they did to him."

"Chits wouldn't have saved him. He made his choice."

"I know that!" She took an audible breath. "Did you find her? Fortuna?"

Thibault shook his head, hiking a thumb over his shoulder at Jupiter. "He says she left this hellhole of her own accord."

"You believe him?"

"Would you?"

Blink said nothing for a moment, then uttered, "No."

She clomped over to Jupiter's sagging form. The vire raised his head when she neared, one eye puffy and swollen, the other bloodshot but alert. "You want Fortuna? Release me, and I will tell you where to find her."

Blink's sloid leaned in. "The only thing I'll release you from is your flesh, bastard. I know Fortuna can't be found any longer."

"What do you know?"

Blink ignored him, turning to Thibault. "You had a job to do, yes?"

Thibault gave her a grim nod and strode forward, flicking back his trench coat. The movement tugged at Jupiter's attention. His remaining good eye widened seeing the reloaded reaver waiting underneath.

In a smooth motion, Thibault slipped it from its sheath and levelled it at Jupiter's head. "I'd tell you to say your prayers, but gods have no deities of their own."

"Wait!" Jupiter flung up both hands. "I'll tell you!"

Thibault's finger hovered at the trigger, desperate for justice. The thought of Fortuna's face froze it fast. "Speak."

"A deal, Allard. A life for a life."

Thibault jammed the reaver barrel into Jupiter's puffed socket. The vire flinched back, but Thibault drove it deeper. "No deals."

Jupiter's chest heaved, his pupils darting for escape. Thibault knew the result. Jupiter would talk. Cowards always did, staring down their ending. Even a blade of grass looks tempting when you're dangling from a cliff.

"It wasn't me," Jupiter said, breathless. "Last time I saw her, she was alive."

"Then who, damn it?" Thibault growled through clenched teeth.

"It wa—"

A crunching pounding rose in the chamber, stifling Jupiter's next words. The sound rolled over them, rising in intensity, echoing out of a corridor. Thibault's heart quickened, his fingers tense around the reaver's stock.

Gleaming crimson sloids flooded through the opening and into the chamber, each one wielding an assault rifle. Anuthuma Blood Fist.

The combat sloids took a bead on them, laser sights glowing fiercely. The squad fanned out, surrounding their small group. Blink's junkyard Reggie clones backed away, pressed together in a tight circle.

Blink's sloid stepped forwards. "What the bloody hell do you want?"

Another crimson sloid marched past the ring of red metal, this one with no weapon. Thibault knew who it was before it even spoke.

"Bravo, hound, bravo! I hadn't expected to hear from you again."

Condrite.

CHAPTER
TWENTY-TWO

The red sloids ringed them like a bloody shield, each rifle trained. Thibault lowered his reaver.

Condrite's sloid swaggered over to Jupiter. "My, my, the great thunder god, on his knees! If only your demented followers could see you now. But they've fled, haven't they, my lord?" Condrite chuckled, sounding like a sputtering engine. "You thought you were safe from me, huddling in your Barren." He spied the wrecked nullifier overhead. "That looks like an electrical strike, don't you think? Was the Lord of Lightning brought low by his own hand? Shocking!"

Jupiter fixed his lone good eye on the mocking sloid. "I think you lied when you said she meant nothing to you."

Thibault shot a look at Jupiter. She? Did he mean Fortuna?

Condrite only chortled, leaning back with full-bodied laughter. "You both mean less than a speck of shit to me, but we must have our amusements, mustn't we? You're the most fun I've had in decades, Wode!"

Wode? That name sounded familiar . . .

"It's Jupiter now, asshole."

"Yes!" Condrite guffawed. "Just Jupiter! How far you've fallen, Wode. Like a rigid turd, plopping into the water from on high." The red sloid leaned in, Condrite's tone becoming vicious. "And you thought to fuck with me, turd? Bribe me with my own possessions?"

He was talking about Fortuna. Thibault frowned at Jupiter. "So you did end her."

His gaze flicked to Thibault. "Not me, idiot." Then it drifted back to Condrite's sloid. "Him."

Blink's motley sloid stamped forward, causing the ring of crimson Blood Fist to tense. She stabbed a finger at Condrite. "It was you, you bastard! Your own wife? Why?"

"I recognise that tone . . ." Condrite's sloid tapped a digit on its visor. "Mechanic! Is that you in there?" He swept an arm around the chamber, gesturing at the cluster of Reggie clones. "These are your children, I take it?"

"We are not children, sir." The Reggies spoke in perfect synchrony. "And we will not allow you to harm Madam."

"Allow?" Condrite pursed his lips. He turned away, striding to the encircling reds, and snatched a rifle from the nearest one. "Give me that!"

Thibault could feel Condrite's sleazy smirk from behind the visor. The rifle cracked with burst fire, three shots slamming into the nearest Reggie. The blue Ortrea helm shredded under the impact, the bearer staggering back, toppling with a loud crash.

"Hold what, sweet cheeks?" Condrite levelled the rifle at Blink's sloid. "You got some backtalk for me too?"

Before Blink could retort, Thibault held out his hands, reaver pointed at the ceiling, finger off the trigger. "Easy. You got what you wanted." He gestured to Jupiter. "Here he is. The thunder god himself."

Condrite didn't lower the rifle. "Do you recall my instructions to you, hound?"

Thibault didn't reply. He knew what was coming next.

The red sloid flipped the rifle, catching it by the barrel. It thrust the weapon forward, offering it to Thibault. "Make good on your commitment, Allard. No payment without a reckoning."

Thibault stared at the rifle butt, jet metal with a grooved plastic stock. More of Condrite's little games. The weapon was nothing compared to the firepower arrayed around them. Never mind that Thibault, Tyre and Jupiter were the only flesh vire in the chamber. The only ones with something to lose.

Thibault holstered his reaver and grabbed the rifle, metal cool under his chrome palm.

"What did you do to her?" Blink's suppressed fury infected her tone, even modified by the sloid's speakers. "You know you'll enjoy the telling, boy."

"Boy, is it?" Condrite giggled. "But you're right, of course. I *will* enjoy this story." His sloid aimed a kick at Jupiter's ribs, making the muscled vire grunt. "Why don't you start, Brian?"

Brian Wode. The name tolled in Thibault's mind like the last puzzle piece slotting into place. A tech billionaire before the Bloodscourge, always in the media feeds, always spouting the news of his own glory.

Jupiter stared back at Condrite, saying nothing. Thibault could feel the hate radiating off him like a heat wave.

"Lost for words all of a sudden? I guess it must be hard, falling so low. Allow me to enlighten them on your behalf." The sloid's helm swung to Thibault. "You're going to enjoy this, hound. Listen close." Condrite took an exaggerated breath. "What if I told you Jupiter's *Fourth* is really Jupiter's *Third*? And, in fact, not even Jupiter's at all?"

Thibault frowned. Jupiter's Third? What did that mean? A play on words? They were called the Fourth because Jupiter was arrogant enough to consider his little group one of the Trinity. A fourth branch. If they were the Third instead . . .

Realisation struck like a coiled fist. Thibault tasted ash. "Jupiter works for one of the Trinity."

"Brilliant, hound! A brilliant mind! You only had to be led there by the nose!" The sloid's metal hands clapped together with a clang. "Jupiter is an Isos lieutenant. The Lightning Lord is Golden Army, through and through." Condrite waved an arm around the gold-plated chamber. "Easy to miss, of course."

Jupiter glowered at Condrite from beneath his chiselled brow.

Condrite continued. "The Fourth is little more than a honey trap for thralls. Needy vire join his flock, hoping to escape the contracts of the Trinity, and he siphons them off to Isos termini. The great Brian Wode: entrepreneur extraordinaire, darling of the A-list, most fortuitous of the Fortune 500." His voice deepened to a growl. "Suckling the leavings from the golden cock of the Isos Family, desperate for scraps from the big table."

"Fuck. You." A vein pulsed in Jupiter's neck.

The sloid's backlit visor angled to Thibault. "The fool thought to use my wife as a bargaining chip, to play Anuthuma against Isos and increase his percentage." Condrite laughed. "A stratagem worthy of the old world, old boy, but not the new one."

"And you betrayed me, bastard." Jupiter growled from the floor. "Tried to end your own wife in front of me."

"You can't betray your enemies, dolt." Condrite backhanded Jupiter across the face, spattering the flagstones with black blood. "But yes, I was mightily upset when you escaped our meet with the bitch still intact."

He faced Thibault again. "So, Jupiter here concocted another plan for my wench. Fortuna isn't her real name, you see." Condrite paused. "Her name . . . was *Angela*." The word slid off his tongue like grease. "You recognise it, hound?"

Thibault's mouth went dry, desolate as a desert. His heart lurched at the name. Because he did recognise it. The pieces of the puzzle thudded together like a sealed tomb.

"Jupiter sent her to an Isos terminus." Thibault barely whispered the words.

Condrite giggled. "Yes indeed! I see you've finally worked it out. So clever, hunter, so clever when you're told all the clues! But I could not take her back myself, though, could I? There are rules. A balance of power between the three Families. We do not steal each other's property. None of us want a repeat of the Sloid Wars. Bad for business. But there is one hunter out there who stalks the night for the Trinity, feared by wary and unwary alike. A hunter who can seek any game, any prize. Even"—giggles erupted from Condrite—"even from a terminus."

Vomit rushed up from Thibault's stomach, thundering into his mouth like a repulsive typhoon. He clenched his augmented fists so hard he thought he'd warp the metal, swallowing the filth back down. Someone gripped his shoulder, metal fingers digging into the muscle. Blink. It hurt, but he didn't stop her. He deserved it.

"What does he mean?" Blink hissed.

Thibault tried to speak the words, but they came out hoarse, unformed.

Condrite filled the void. "I contracted your alloy-armed friend there to fetch her for me, Mechanic. Like an obedient dog, he did as asked. And got paid in full, I might add."

"And you ended her." Blink's grip tightened, making Thibault's knees weak. The rifle clattered to the floor, his fingers limp.

Condrite's voice darkened. "I sat in judgement. I found her wanting."

"You bastard."

Was she talking to Condrite? Or to Thibault?

Perhaps both.

Fortuna's face bled into view, pleading with Thibault from atop the Veeshield. *I need to know if . . .* he *found me.*

Condrite hadn't found her. Thibault had. And he'd delivered her right back to the clutches of her abuser. He'd been hunting himself through this rotten city. A mouse in a maze, chasing its own tail, all the exits sabotaged.

"You knew all along." Thibault stared into Condrite's visor, his eyes trying to delve into the oily slime within. "This was just another game to you."

"Oh, no, no, no, it was no game, Allard, no game at all." The sloid stepped forward, leaning in. "Do you know what I hate more than anything? More than anything in the world, old or new?" The sloid's helm cocked to one side. "Hope, Allard. I fucking *despise* hope. Hope has no place in this stinking cesspit of a city, this boiled blister on the puckered anus of the universe. I have seen it in you, Allard, seen its fingers winding around your heart, whispering sweet lies that you might see your precious Marina once more."

Condrite's voice became a quiet hiss. "I will crush that vile hope, because it does not belong in this world. Can you see, now, where you truly live?"

Thibault stared into the sloid's visor, an incomprehensible stream of glowing characters rushing down the glass. He saw his own face reflected there, a mirror into his soul. The words tumbled from his mouth before he could think to claw them back. "Because your daughter died before the Bloodscourge?" Thibault heard Condrite take a sharp breath through the sloid's speaker. "Because she died right before she could be Turned and saved?"

The arm struck out from nowhere, hammering into Thibault's cheek, almost sending him sprawling. The flavour of ash filled his mouth, the taste of dried bones and desiccated skin. He'd hit his mark, all right.

"Clever, dog. Very clever. You are correct, of course. I will not allow goodness to exist in a world denied to my daughter." Condrite chuckled with all the mirth of a maniac. "But our little game isn't over yet." His hand snapped out, grasped Jupiter's head and twisted it to face Thibault. "Finish your turn."

Thibault met Jupiter's eyes, saw the resignation in them. "No."

The snigger that emitted from the sloid's speakers started slowly, building faster and faster, deep enough with bass that it distorted into static. "Not even . . . for Marina?"

Hearing her name on the snake's lips made Thibault close his eyes. Marina was the morsel on the end of everyone's hook, the bait he couldn't resist. For a moment, when he'd decided to return and help Tyre, he'd thought maybe this once, just maybe, he could be more. If only for a brief time.

"Don't play his game." Tyre croaked like a decomposing corpse. The brute's face was pallid, sick with pain, but his gaze snagged something in Thibault's soul. "Let me do it. I owe that bastard."

Tyre rolled, groaning. He tried to stand but fell down again.

Condrite tutted. "No, hunter. Even if that oversized cadaver limps over here, the task is yours. Yours alone."

Thibault trudged forward, his feet carrying him of their own accord. He lifted the assault rifle from the floor, eased the barrel into his left hand, found the trigger nub with ease. Jupiter's bloodshot eye stared back.

"Stop, boyo . . ." Tyre wheezed.

Tyre didn't understand. If Condrite knew where Thibault could find Marina, he had no choice.

Jupiter spoke through gritted teeth. "You're a thrall too, Allard. Just without the mesh."

"We're all thralls," Thibault whispered.

He squeezed the trigger.

CHAPTER
TWENTY-THREE

Aurora hadn't changed. Not that Thibault had expected anything different.

The night was clear, offering an unobstructed view of the star-ridden sky, Nova breathing below. The city felt like it was waiting. Calm. Expectant. Even the music from the dawnclub at Thibault's back sounded duller, muffled like a slug shot through a silencer.

It had taken a long time to crawl out of Olympus. He'd stayed behind after Condrite and his sloids left, the enforcer's cackling leaving echoes like footprints in wet cement. Condrite had tossed Thibault a handful of chits, most of them landing in the growing pool of Jupiter's blood.

Come and see him, Condrite had said. Come and see him, and he'd tell Thibault of his wife. Thibault rushed at Condrite, demanded the information, but the Blood Fist sloids clubbed him down until consciousness threatened to disappear altogether.

Blink hadn't spoken to Thibault again. She'd instructed the Reggies to carry both Tyre and his brother's corpse back to the surface, but left Thibault where he lay. She turned at the exit, her thoughts unreadable and unspoken. Her sloid shook its head and left, the Reggies trailing behind with their cargo.

Thibault sat on his knees in the chamber for a long time, the ashen scent of Jupiter's blood and his own mixing in his nostrils. He hadn't wanted to leave. He'd known the path to the surface would lead him back here. To the slip. To Aurora.

He hoped Fortuna wouldn't come. He hoped she'd found peace somehow in the meantime, been deconstructed back into the slip's code, the anomaly of her chance existence corrected. It wouldn't make him feel less guilty, but at least he wouldn't have to face her, admit what he'd done.

Odd, that he hadn't considered not coming. Was he trying to be honourable? Now? After what he'd done to her? He was a fool.

Thibault's stomach felt like a stone, a heavy weight dragging him down. He just needed to find Marina, and then he could let all this go, be free of it. Couldn't he? Or would he haul it with him, his luggage of sin, bigger every passing night?

He sensed the spectre before she made a sound. There was no physical hint, but the back of his neck shivered, and his heart dropped into his boots.

"Did you find out who ended me?" Fortuna's voice rose behind him, as strong as he remembered. "Did Condrite find me?"

Thibault hesitated before turning around. He could exit now. Leave the slip, leave her voice to speak alone into the night.

But he couldn't do it. Her tone had already captured him, that courage tugging at his ragged conscience.

He turned, met her gaze. Her green eyes were wide, her hands rubbing together like they didn't know how to be still. She wanted to know that Condrite hadn't found her. That was what she wanted Thibault to say.

He could say that. Lie to her. Lie to set her at ease.

Why did his guilt draw the line there?

"He found you, kin."

Her face twitched.

"Condrite found you . . . because of me. Jupiter dumped you in an Isos terminus, and Condrite paid me to bring you out and return you to him."

Her face dropped finally, every fine muscle slackening as the hope drained from it, understanding stealing it away. Disbelief took over next, the possibility that Thibault might be lying flitting over her features, until eventually acceptance came, and with it, anger.

"You . . . took me to him?"

Thibault nodded, forcing himself to meet her gaze. "I did. I know it isn't worth much, but I'm sorry. I didn't know."

"Didn't know."

"I didn't recognise you. Your face here, it's different. Not the face I saw. Because of what Blink . . ." He trailed off.

"I never grew accustomed to my new face," Fortuna said softly. "Had my old one too long for my mind to let it go, I think. So here I am, trapped as I was before."

"Why—" Thibault choked on the next words, then steadied himself. "Why me? Why did you find me, ask for my help?"

"I think," Fortuna said, shaking her head, "I think I knew. I think I knew you'd found me, taken me back to him. I was so compelled to ask you for help—I thought if anyone could reverse what had been done . . ." Her voice hardened. "And then I saw you in your echo, with your wife. I thought you were someone I could rely upon."

Something hit the ground at her feet. Wet drops, sliding down her cheeks.

Spectral tears.

How could a program's crying wrench at him so?

"I'm sorry," Thibault said again.

Empty. Useless.

Those tear-laden eyes fixed on him. He flinched from the anger he saw there, the pain he'd caused.

"I hope," Fortuna said in a thick voice, "you *never* find your wife."

The words knifed through him, shredding the final tatters that remained of his soul. He opened his mouth to apologise again, to plead, to say how sorry he was, but the words died on his tongue, worthless and wasted.

Fortuna flickered, then disappeared, porting somewhere else. One moment there, the next gone. Like she'd never been.

Where did spectres go? Did they roam the slip until someone finally pulled the plug on it? Or did they fade away, recombined, reused, reincarnated?

Thibault hoped it was the latter.

He pulled his trench tighter, but he wasn't cold. He turned and sped towards his exit and the meeting with Condrite, his heart solidifying like tempered steel.

He'd been a damned fool. He knew that now.

The person he'd imagined, standing tall and proud like the man he'd been before the Bloodscourge, saving Tyre, helping Fortuna—it had all been a trick his mind played on itself to spare him from the truth.

He could never be that man again.

That hope had been a mirage.

EPILOGUE

Thibault's reflection rippled over the facade of dark glass fronting Anuthuma Skytower, fitting his form to the sleek shape of the Trinity eyesore. The colossal sunscraper speared upwards, hammering through the Veeshield dome far overhead, stretching toward the distant stars.

A squad of crimson Blood Fist sloids guarded the entrance, gleaming like they hadn't seen action since the Sloid Wars. Their pulsing visors watching Thibault's approach with a complete lack of concern, assault rifles still adhered to their thigh plates. One of them raised a shining red hand when he neared. The digits flared in warning.

"The fuck do you want, meat?" The modulation algorithm over the pilot's voice speckled the sound with static.

Thibault noted the pilot's handle glowing in the corner of its visor: [*Firestorm*]. Real friendly. A waterfall of cryptic characters cascaded down the faceplate, the glowing output vomiting a wealth of incomprehensible system data.

Thibault met the sloid's stare. "Condrite wants to see me."

"Hot date, huh?" A few of the other sloids snickered.

Thibault could feel the smug sneer from the pilot, but he held back a retort. Threatening Blood Fist was a fast way to secure a slow ending. Instead, Thibault remained quiet and waited.

Firestorm sniffed with digital disdain and turned toward the revolving doors. "Follow meat, and don't get lost. If you're lying to me …"

Thibault fell in behind the crimson sloid, winging around the other Blood Fist goons. He tailed Firestorm through the revolving doors. Inside, more of the gleaming soldiers lined the lobby, a row of red statues ready to rain death on the enemies of the Anuthuma.

Firestorm led them across the polished marble floor and through a pair of glass doors to the corridor leading to Condrite's offices. Outside, Firestorm rapped metal knuckles on the mahogany.

A muted reply sounded beyond. "What the fuck is it now?"

Apparently, that was a sufficient response to gain entry. Firestorm swung the door open and swept into the room, the sloid's rubber soles scuffing the carpet.

Condrite leaned back in an oversized executive chair, slick-blonde hair so oiled the down-lights lent it a golden sheen. He sat before a wide, transparent desk made of a single sheet of polycarbonate curved at the ends to form legs. An array of different powders coated surface, lit from below by an interface built-in to the plastic. Thibault recognised a few of them by the hue alone, but others could have been anything.

In the crazed nights and years following the Bloodscourge, there'd been a mad chemical frenzy to find a drug capable of taming the Thirst. Some offered euphoria, others an existential or hallucinatory distraction, but none truly quelled the insatiable beast raging within. Hush, rid-v, splash, atom, dred. All names for the failed experiments littering Condrite's desk. Slake had been the last—and most successful—of the chemical attempts, because the only thing that eased the Thirst was a total absence of thought.

Then came the Feast. And the world changed anew.

"Allard!" Condrite spread his hands in mock greeting. "Took your time in showing up. You've saved me from ordering my reds out to fetch you, though I'm sure they're mighty disappointed, aren't you, Fireshorts?"

"It's Firestorm, sir."

"Just piss off, would you?" Condrite waved a lazy hand. "There's a dear."

Thibault kept his face impassive. Condrite could taunt the Blood Fist without repercussions, but that power didn't extend beyond. If he grinned now, it would cause trouble, or pain, or both.

The enforcer's blonde head dove into the pile of powders, snorting several colours. His nose came away caked in random narcotics, no telling what he'd fed into his bloodstream. Wiping the back of his hand past his nose, he settled back with a sigh, pupils so wide his irises disappeared.

"I did what you wanted." Thibault forced the words out. "Now tell me where I can find my wife."

Condrite steepled his fingers, smirking with all the class of an oily rag. "Not even a 'please'?"

Thibault swallowed back both bile and pride. "Please."

"I don't think I could ever tire of hearing that from you, Allard. Say it again."

Thibault took a step forward, his whole body quivering with suppressed tension. *"Tell. Me."*

The faintest kiss of air at the nape of Thibault's neck told him someone else had entered the room. Condrite's eyes widened and the blonde vire straightened in his chair. Thibault froze at the enforcer's rigid posture, holding his breath.

A feminine voice purred in Thibault's ear. "You don't make demands, hound."

Thibault didn't turn. Didn't move. Didn't need to. He knew who it was. Zither. Known by many simply as the Ender, because that was her skill. Thibault had worked hard to avoid her.

He heard a soft decompression accompanied by a gentle whirr. A black, segmented blade snaked through the air before his face, undulating to an unheard song. It flashed for his neck. The edge kissed his throat, cold metal pushing up against his chin, lifting his head back. He felt the sharp sting of the blade slicing the surface of his skin.

"A good hound does as instructed. No more. No less." Zither rounded in front of him, a pair of optical mods pulsing bright red behind her pupils. The wingblade hinged at her shoulder. The only pieces of her that weren't black were her white hair and pale skin. "Are you a good hound?"

Thibault held her gaze over the bridge of his nose. "We made a bargain, kin, Condrite and I. I've delivered. He has not."

Zither hissed, wove in close. Close enough, he could smell her sour breath. "I've heard of you, dog." The blade left his neck, reappearing an instant later in front of his face, joined by a twin arcing out of her opposite shoulder. Each blade pointed at one of his eyes. "Lucy and Vanessa have been desperate to meet you."

"Can't say the same."

Her fingers danced on the nanofilm coating his chrome forearms—his left arm repaired from the damage inflicted by Jupiter only an hour ago. She latched onto his elbows and pulled him in. Her fangs glinted, framing a sultry sneer. "One of these nights, I'll twist these pretty arms from their sockets, carve the leftovers into neat little slices, throw them to the skinners to fight over."

Thibault tried to clamp his lips shut to prevent the taunt clamouring for a voice. But he failed. "I won't be so creative. I'll just end you."

The hovering spikes dove for his eyeballs. Then stopped. So near they were all he could see. So near, the tips must almost have been touching his squishy orbs.

"Shall I pluck them out?" Zither whispered. "Leave you to wander the night, lost and blind?"

"I'm already lost, kin, blind or no."

She giggled like he'd made a cute joke. Maybe he had, because the next moment the blades wove away, realigning with her arms and coupling back together with a chorus of clicks. They seated into the upper side of limbs, perfectly formed, as good as any work Blink could do. Her voice became louder, rougher. "Show the dog his woman. Time is short."

Condrite's smile faded at the Ender's order, though Thibault noticed he hid his sour expression from the dark-clad woman. "You want to see your wife, Allard?" The enforcer's fingers tapped a quick pattern on the glass desk, backlit controls pulsing at the touch. "Here's your prize."

Without warning, the opposite wall inverted, plunging from hospital to impenetrable black, like the vacuum of space itself had suddenly invaded. It flickered for a moment, then unfurled an instant later, revealing a wide scene. The entire facade was a single viewing screen, mounted wall-to-wall. It was like they all stood in a three-sided room, the fourth surface opening out into a cavernous space.

Hundreds of slip pods populated the frame, arranged into neat columns and rows. Atop each pod sat a glowing monitor, small islands of light lost in a sordid sea.

A terminus, fit to bursting with thralls, every one meshed.

Thibault's heart teetered on the verge of a bottomless void. Marina was down there somewhere. He knew it for a certainty, even before he could pick her out.

The viewport arced, diving in a sinuous line, the thralls weaving closer. He felt his stomach revolt from the angle, his sense of orientation foiled by the perspective. His breathing quickened, racing in time with the beating in his chest.

Then he saw.

Her pale face was calm in repose, matted hair clumping

around the plastic mesh fused to her head. A thin hospital gown covered her body, bare arms and legs exposed. The camera halted above the pod, offering Thibault an unobstructed view of the sight he'd sought for so long. His wife. Marina. Trapped in her thraldom and him on the outside.

Adrenaline imploded inside, surging through his veins with nowhere to go. It left him sweating, shivering, soulless. Thibault took a step forward, his arm rising of its own volition.

The wall blanked out, becoming stale white once more.

"No!" Thibault rushed forwards, a roaring in his ears. "No!"

A dark shape blurred. Lights exploded. His back smacked the floor.

Thibault wheezed through decompressed lungs, struggling to suck in air. His attacker loomed over him, the fist that had clubbed him still curled. Zither's snarling visage snapped into focus.

Thibault's voice was strained and hoarse. "Where is she? What terminus is it?"

She kneeled, leaning an elbow on her leg. "I told the Altus I could do this job, but you know what he said?" She smiled, fangs bright. "He said I was the Ender for a reason, and this thing, he needs alive. Can you guess what he wants, hound?"

Thibault barely heard her, his mind still full of what he'd seen, picking apart the clues. "That could have been a recording. How do I know you still have her?"

"We have her. That's all you need to know."

Thibault tried to sit up, but Zither's augmented arm slammed into his chest, hammering him back into the carpet. His skull blossomed with pain for a second time.

He stared up, gripping her leg, feeling the hard metal beneath. How much of this creature was augmented?

Condrite appeared behind Zither, staring down with a sleazy smile. "Just one more task, Allard, and you may see her again."

Just one more. Always, just one more.

"Give me the damned job." The words tasted like ash on his tongue. "I'll do what needs doing."

"Of course you will." Condrite's smile widened. "Your crispy friend has stepped on the wrong toes." He chuckled, but the sound held no mirth. "The Altus wants Ors. He wants you to snare the Scorched."

ENTER THE SLIP

Join the Trinity.

Sign up for news, special deals and release notifications
simontull.com/join

SIMON**TULL**

ACKNOWLEDGMENTS

Writing is solitary work, but publishing a book is not. Without the help of the people mentioned below, *A Mirage in the Memory* would have been a pale shadow of what it is now.

First, I have to thank my wife, Sylvie, for reading my words long before they became whole. Your unwavering support made this possible. Most of all, thank you for telling me when my writing sucked.

Finding people willing to read your work and give you honest feedback can be tough, but writing communities like Scribophile make it much easier. I want to thank everyone who critiqued my work, including Jay Klements and Bern Michaels. I'd like to thank Bern in particular for the detailed, enthusiastic, and often hilarious comments of the entire novella.

I also have to thank my Friday writing group (in alphabetical order to avoid fisticuffs)—Connie Smith, Craig Scutt (aka The Flying Scuttsman), Sasha Stella, Siobhan Kavanagh and others—for your thorough, insightful critiques, and overall enthusiasm.

Finally, I want to thank Dylan Garity for his help with tasering my many writing tics, his focused edits, and great suggestions, plus Jenny DePierre for her laser-focused proofing.

Each of you helped me understand both my strengths and weaknesses as a writer and helped me make *A Mirage in the Memory* real.

Thank you.

SIMON**TULL**

Simon Tull is a software sorcerer by day and a couch potato by night. By the cold light of morning, he transforms coffee grounds into fun stories. On the rare occasions he's able to do something other than sling code or sweat words, he fancies himself as a yoga student, basketballer, runner, cook, and fussy cat companion.

Like many science fiction and fantasy authors, Simon was inspired to write his own stories after vicariously experiencing the exploits of Rand al'Thor, Druss the Legend, Murderbot, and, of course, Arthur Dent.

He lives on the Bellarine Peninsula in Victoria, Australia with his wife and cat.

Delve deeper into the slip at
`simontull.com`